Holiday Home

A Windsor Peak Novella

Book 4.5

Denise Latham

ISBN: 979-8-9888952-6-8

Cover design by Book Designs by Shae.

Editing by Nina Fiegl, Romance Editor.

www.deniselatham.com

Dedication

To the readers. Those of you who have been here since book one, and new readers who are picking this up because they are Christmas book fanatics like me.

All of you who are reading my books, sending encouraging messages, sharing my name with friends, and who have fallen as in love with Windsor Peak as I have. You are making my dreams come true. Thank you all.

I hope you have a magical holiday season and a wonderful new year!

Chapter 1

Holly Kerrigan was thoroughly annoyed. She had arrived at the airport with plenty of time to get on her flight to Vermont but had been delayed going through TSA as they paused to let someone important through security without the regular people watching. Why they couldn't just fly private rather than holding everyone else up was beyond her, but that delay meant she barely had enough time to grab her Starbucks before getting on board. And she needed the coffee more than she needed her next breath, so she was willing to risk waiting in the long line and then having to run to the jetway. When they finally called her name, she grabbed the Venti cup with her name and a little Christmas tree on the side and turned to dash to her gate.

Only to come up short because a man had come to stand directly behind her, causing her to stumble and spill the coffee all down the front of her pants and sweater. "What the—" she gasped as the hot liquid hit her skin.

"Oh," he said, looking her up and down. "That's unfortunate."

"Unfortunate?" she nearly screeched, staring at him in disbelief. "This is your fault."

He was wearing a hat pulled low and sunglasses, despite the dim lighting in the hall. His beard was big and bushy, and his oversize hoodie hid most of his body. Despite not being able to see most of his face, she could feel his gaze sweep over her again. "Looks to me like you're a bit clumsy," he said. "Excuse me, my coffee is ready."

She glared at him as he disappeared, having given no further thought to her situation. The barista handed her a wad of napkins and a new coffee, giving her a sympathetic look before turning back to the next customer. Holly checked her watch, realizing she didn't have enough time to duck into the bathroom and change into the clothes she had in her carry-on. It was either change and miss the flight or make the flight but go soaking wet.

The flight attendant did a double take as she scanned her ticket in. "What happened to you?"

"Coffee accident," she said. "Luckily, it's a short flight from New York to Vermont. I can change when I get there."

"You might want to change on the plane," she said with a laugh. "Otherwise, the clothes will freeze right on your skin when you land. Did you see the temperature?"

"I did," she said with a groan. "But my sister is a new mom, and my parents are flying in. It's also my birthday, so even if I wanted to skip it, they wouldn't let me. On the bright side, at least I'll have a white Christmas."

"Merry Christmas, and Happy Birthday," the agent said with a smile.

Holly started down the jetway, shivering when the cool air hit the wet clothes against her skin. She was likely the last person to board, but with how much she traveled, she knew how close she could cut it. Her aisle seat was reserved, and her small tote would fit in the overhead or under the seat in front of her. The small plane only held about twenty passengers, so it wasn't as difficult to find space for her bag as her full flight from Nevada had been.

Holly was settled into her seat and putting in her AirPods when she realized the coffee-spiller had boarded the plane. He was escorted to the empty first row of the plane by two flight attendants, who then waited for him to pull items out of his bag before lifting them into the overhead compartment for him. They were both smiling down at him, virtually beaming at the jerk who had felt no remorse over causing her to nearly burn herself. Not to mention, boarding a flight with soaking wet clothes. Fortunately, she was several rows back and decided she could close her eyes and ignore his existence for the short flight. Once they were in Vermont, she would never see him again.

When the plane landed, the same two flight attendants jumped up to get his bags down and guided him to the door. She looked at her fellow passengers, wondering if anyone else was witnessing this, but they were all busy grabbing their own items and putting on jackets. She shook her head and joined the line to get off the plane, wishing the crew a happy holiday on the way by. Fortunately, she had used the tiny bathroom just after takeoff to change into the extra set of leggings and long-sleeve shirt she had tucked into her carry-on, so she was dry, but likely to be freezing unless she could pull a sweater out of her checked suitcase.

She followed the small crowd to the baggage claim area, choosing a spot where she could easily see the bags coming but wouldn't block anyone else. When the alarm sounded and the belt started to move, everyone inevitably took a step forward, filling in the small space. The first bag came through, and her carry on was sent flying as the owner tried to get through to grab it. "Hey," she cried out, scrambling to tuck things back into the tote. Glancing up once she had secured everything, she realized it was the same guy. He clearly needed a lesson in personal space and kindness, especially at this time of year.

"You know—" she started to say as he turned back to walk away.

"Sorry, I can't," he mumbled, looking at the floor. He walked away quickly with his bags, leaving her standing with her mouth open, staring at his back. She had never encountered such rudeness before. He clearly had no Christmas spirit, she decided.

She turned back just in time to watch her bag passing by and groaned. Now she would have to wait for it to go all the way around, when all she wanted was to be free from the airport. She pulled out her cell phone and sent a quick text to her sister, who was outside waiting for her. Shea responded quickly, assuring her it was no rush. Holly saw her bag come back around and grabbed it without issue this time. She opted to head out to the car rather than pull out something warm to put on, wanting to see her sister quickly. A decision she quickly regretted when the doors opened, sending in a swirl of freezing cold air and snow.

Shea was standing outside, the back of an SUV open, smiling widely and waving to her. "Holly!"

"Hi," she said, hugging her sister tight. "I'm so happy to see you."

"You must be freezing," Shea said. "Get in the car and warm up. Isobel is at home with Jake, she was napping so I couldn't bring her with me."

"Oh, that stinks," she sighed. "I need to meet my niece!"

"I know, but you're here for two weeks," Shea said. "You'll have plenty of cuddle time with her."

Holly climbed into the passenger seat, putting her hands in front of the heat vents. Shea jumped in behind the wheel and pulled away, smiling over at her as she did. "I'm so excited that you're here," she said. "I can't believe it's been a year since we saw you."

"I know," Holly said. "It's been such a busy year. I'm so grateful for Facetime, so I could see you and your big belly. And of course, to see Izzie."

"Mom and Dad already landed," Shea told her. "We're having a big dinner tonight at Patrick's house, I hope you're up for it?"

"Up for dinner at a celebrity's house? I think I can manage," Holly laughed.

"He has Natalie Cloud staying with him," Shea said. "And Liam Dorsey arrived yesterday, I think. Patrick takes them all in like orphans at Christmas."

"You said Natalie was having a rough year," Holly said. "How is she doing?"

"Not great," Shea shared. "That's why Liam was coming, really. They all rally around her. Filming all those superhero movies together all these years has made them a little family. Zane wasn't able to make it, although he wanted to come. His family is close and wanted him back in Scotland. But it was nice of Liam to come."

"Just so I'm clear," Holly laughed. "I came to Vermont for a quiet family holiday in a sleepy small town, and I'm going to be surrounded by celebrities?"

Shea nodded. "That about sums it up."

"Perfect. When does Rex arrive?"

"Tomorrow," Shea said. "Patrick arranged for a private flight."

"The dog has a better arrangement than I did. I should have hitched a flight with him," she said. "This is what I get for planning a few days in New York before coming here."

"All that matters is you're here now," Shea said. "And I'm so glad."

Holly's bad mood edged away, her sister's gentleness and good nature soothing away the annoyances of the day. Her holiday spirit was slowly returning, because Shea's enthusiasm about Izzie's first Christmas was infectious. She listened as her sister went on about the plans for the upcoming weeks and gushed about her new daughter and husband. As she went on, Holly couldn't help but think that Christmas in Vermont might be exactly what she needed.

***

Hours spent cuddling baby Izzie and hearing about her nephew Charlie's exploits in high school continued to raise her spirits. Her brother-in-law Jake arrived home from work, having spent the day surveying several construction projects he was the contractor for. When he arrived, he seemed quiet and withdrawn, and Shea pulled him into their bedroom after a short time with his daughter. When she emerged ten minutes later, she was alone and frowning.

"Everything okay?" Holly asked as Shea sank down next to her on the couch. Charlie had long since disappeared, stating he had homework to do, but Holly suspected that was code for video games to play. She didn't blame him, not many sixteen-year-olds wanted to hang out with the aunt they had only met a few times. Charlie was Shea's stepson, his own mother had died in a terrorist attack when he was an infant. The incident had spurred Jake to enlist in the military, leaving Charlie behind to be raised by his grandfather. Despite Shea loving him, no one felt it was right for her to adopt him and replace his mom fully. Holly loved seeing their relationship, though, knowing that Charlie loved her sister and was happy to have a stable family life.

"He's tired," Shea explained of Jake. "And he had a bad day. It triggers his PTSD, he can be crabby and snap at people. He will be better after he has a little alone time and maybe a nap."

"This is what Rex will help with," Holly said. "Help calm him down and recognize the triggers so he can provide comfort."

"I'm so curious to see how it works," Shea said. "We had never thought of a service dog until you suggested it, and I'm so glad you did. While he's resting, do you want to help me put together what I'm bringing to Patrick's?"

The two sisters busied themselves with putting the cookies Shea had baked onto a festive tray, and all the things that Izzie would require to be out of the house for a few hours. Fortunately, she was an easy baby and only needed a few extra blankets and her pajamas so she could sleep in her portable crib. By the time they were done, Charlie and Jake had joined them, Jake looking better.

"Everyone ready to go?" Jake asked as he and his son gathered the bags. "Holly, I'd like to walk if you don't mind, but Charlie wants to drive if you're game to supervise. Then all this gear can go in the car."

"You got your permit?" Holly hip bumped the teenager. "Congrats."

"I did. A little late because I was so busy with hockey and work all summer, but I finally got it." He grinned at her, clearly proud of himself. "I haven't been able to drive much because Dad and Shea won't let me drive with Izzie in the car."

"Alright, I'll be your teacher while I'm here," she promised. They said goodbye and headed out to Jake's SUV, Charlie jingling the keys in his hand. When they got in and he turned the radio to a rock station, she laughed and switched to a channel playing Christmas music. "You need to be focused on the road, my friend. Not rocking out."

He rolled his eyes but nodded, putting the car into drive. "Can we do a lap around town before we go to Patrick's? It will take Dad and Shea a little while to walk there anyway."

"Sure," she said. "Go for it."

She spent the next thirty minutes clinging to the door handle while trying to bite her tongue, sure that there would be no mailboxes left standing by the time Charlie got his license. How he managed to avoid crashing into everything on the right side of the car was beyond her, and she sighed with relief when they drove up the long road to Patrick's property.

She had visited the house the year before but was still in awe at the size of it. Patrick was a famous actor, and the house represented his success. It was a huge, farmhouse style mansion. A large stable was behind the driveway, where Patrick kept rescue horses, and beyond that Holly knew a guest cabin was nestled. The house was lit up with Christmas lights, and smoke billowed from the chimney.

"I did okay, right?" Charlie asked as he slid the car into park.

"You did great, bud," she said. "We'll work on it for the next few weeks while I'm here. You'll get even better, I promise."

"You look a little pale," Charlie said as they walked towards the house. "You sure I was okay?"

"It's been a long day," she said. "It started when some jerk made me spill coffee all over myself, and I almost missed my flight. Now I just need a glass of wine and to relax, it wasn't your driving at all."

"You're nice when you lie," he said, grinning at her as he pushed the door open.

Holly spotted her parents sitting in chairs next to Jake and Shea in the large living room, all holding glasses of wine. Jake's older brother Dan and his wife Kendra, along with their seven-year-old daughter Calle, were seated on one couch. Jake's father Ben and his wife Stella were on the opposite couch, holding the two babies and beaming as their grandson Charlie entered. Patrick's girlfriend Emma and her sister Zoe were in the open kitchen, and paused to wave to her as she came in. The rest of the family called out greetings as her own parents jumped up to hug her and welcome her to Vermont. Jake's younger brother

Patrick gave her a quick hug before pressing a glass of wine into her hand.

"I drove with him yesterday," he whispered as he hugged her. "I think you need this."

"Thanks." She laughed. "After the day I've had, this is perfect."

"We're just waiting on Natalie, who likes to make an entrance, and Liam," Patrick said. "Zoe and Emma are in the kitchen setting up some snacks for everyone. Have you met JJ?" He gestured to the other man in the room, who stood slowly and offered her his hand.

"We haven't met, but I've heard about you," Holly said. She had heard about the local sheriff being shot right here in Patrick's house when he was protecting Natalie. Not only had she heard about it firsthand from Shea, but all the gossip magazines had been going crazy with the story. JJ was married to Emma's sister Zoe, and the photogenic group had been featured on many magazines heralding the local Sheriff's heroism in saving the starlet. "I'm so glad you're doing well."

"Thanks," JJ said. "It's a slow recovery, but I'm getting there. I hope you had a good trip in."

"It's a short flight from New York, but of course there was one jerk to deal with. It happens every holiday season, doesn't it? One guy at the airport who thinks he's more important than everyone else. Unfortunately for me, it meant I flew halfway to Vermont covered in coffee before I was able to change."

"Shame to be so clumsy," a voice said from behind her, causing her to turn and gasp.

Chapter 2

Liam Dorsey studied the woman he had heard talking as he entered the room. Her back was to him, her chestnut-colored hair streaming down her back in loose waves. She looked fit and strong, even from behind. He hadn't really paid attention to her at the airport, assuming that the woman had done the coffee trick on purpose to get him to notice her, but now she was all he could look at. She seemed to light up the room until he spoke and she turned to glare at him.

"You! What are you doing here?" Her eyes shot daggers at him, making him want to retreat into himself. Instead, he donned the familiar elitist actor character he wore so often, leaning against the wall as he allowed his gaze to sweep up her figure. Watching his eyes, her own narrowed and she crossed her arms.

"I'm here to spend Christmas with my friends," he said. "What are you doing here? Did you come to spill something on me now?"

"You're—"

"This is Liam Dorsey," Patrick said, sliding smoothly between them. "Liam, this is Shea's sister Holly."

"Charmed, I'm sure." He smirked at her. "Looking forward to spending the holidays with you." He strolled away from her, moving to pour himself a drink on the bar Patrick had set up.

His friend followed him, with a confused look on his face. "What's up with you and Holly?"

"She bumped into me at the airport in New York," he explained. "Spilled coffee all over herself. I figured it was a ploy to get me to help her, and it would end up being trouble for me. She wasn't happy."

"Doubling down on that seemed like a great idea, I'm sure," Patrick laughed. "But could you try and play nice? She's my family now too, since Jake and Shea are married."

"I'll see what I can do," he promised. "I could be really nice, if you know what I mean."

"Nope," Patrick shook his head. "Holly isn't a vacation hookup. Just be nice."

They both turned as Natalie came down the stairs, with far less fanfare than they were both used to. Her hair was in a ponytail, the blonde she was most known for changed back to her natural reddish hue. Her face was free from makeup, and she wore a simple outfit of jeans and a bulky sweater. She looked nothing like the movie star she was, and he felt his gut churn. Patrick had been talking about how worried he was for weeks, and when Liam had arrived earlier, he had been shocked.

Emma introduced Holly to Natalie, then settled her on the couch between herself and Stella. The women were clearly handling her with kid gloves, and Natalie was allowing herself to coddled. As much as it startled him to see her so off, he was glad she was surrounded by such loving, caring people. If she was in California, she wouldn't be taken care of the way she was here.

Zoe called them all for dinner, and he moved to Nat's side when she stood up, putting an arm around her. "You doing okay?"

"No," she said softly. "I'm really not. But I'm so glad you're here."

"I'd do anything for you," he said, kissing her on the head. "Even though you won't fall in love with me."

She laughed and swatted at him. "Knock it off. I'm not in the mood to flirt."

"I know, but I got you to laugh." He pulled out a chair at the long table for Natalie, then slid out the one next to her for himself, realizing at the last second that Holly was on his other side. She rolled her eyes at him as he sat as if she was annoyed by his nearness. She turned to face Kendra on the other side, virtually putting her back to him, so he spent the meal quietly chatting with Natalie.

Halfway through the meal, JJ excused himself to answer his ringing cell phone. The party continued, the table lively with conversation and laughter, and Liam couldn't help but relax. He had gotten to know Patrick's family over their years of filming a movie series together and enjoyed meeting the new people. Being surrounded by a loving family, and seeing Patrick and his brothers coupled up and clearly happy, gave him a funny feeling that he chose to ignore.

JJ reappeared at the table just before dessert was served, a solemn look on his face. He leaned down and spoke quietly to Patrick and Dan, who were seated next to each other at the opposite end of the table from Liam. Jake, halfway down, threw a roll at them when they continued their whispering. "Hey, this isn't fair. Share with the group."

JJ sighed, staring at Jake. "I didn't want to ruin the mood."

"Spill it," Ben ordered. The father of the three Burrows boys—now grown men—still had the voice of authority that demanded he be obeyed.

"There was a fire at the youth center," JJ said. "Luckily, no one was there. But the damage was significant, and since it happened when the building was empty a full investigation has to happen. Which means insurance will be difficult and won't want to pay for repairs until they know the cause. I'm barely back on desk duty, so I won't be able to do much, but I hate that the kids will be left without a safe place to go during the winter months."

"The youth center offers before and after school activities," Shea shared with the out-of-town guests. "Also provides meals on non-school days, so the kids never go hungry. It's been a major help to our community, donated by our own local hero."

"I can fix it," Patrick said. "Let's get Jake down there and see what we're talking about."

"No one can go in yet," JJ said. "The fire chief has to do his investigation, and it has to be cleared for safety before anyone can get inside. We should wait to see what insurance will pay out."

"But in the meantime, the kids have nowhere to go?" Natalie asked quietly.

"There must be something we can do," Liam said. "I'm happy to help."

"As long as they don't have coffee spilled all over themselves," Holly mumbled, quiet enough that only he heard her.

Before he could respond to the barb, Ben spoke up. "Let's all coordinate tomorrow, see what the situation is and how we can help. The breakfast with Santa will need to be moved, and all these kids now have nowhere to go over the school break for meals. I'm sure we can put our heads together and come up with a safe solution."

When Patrick opened his mouth to speak, Dan quickly cut him off. "Without one person at the table fronting the full cost."

Patrick rolled his eyes and sat back in his chair. "You act like I do it for my ego," he said.

"If it was for ego, Liam would be doing it," Natalie said softly, making the table laugh.

He grinned at her, putting his arm around the back of her chair as he laughed. "We're not ruling that out," he said. "I'll do anything for press. Especially good press."

***

After everyone left, he found Natalie nursing a mug of hot chocolate in front of the fire. The bags under her eyes suggested she wasn't sleeping much, and she was paler than usual. "Talk to me, Nat," he urged as he sat down.

"I wish I could make it better that way," she said with a sad smile. "But I've been doing therapy and talking about it endlessly. It's just a lot, you know?"

A month or so earlier, Natalie had been held at gunpoint at Patrick's house. A crazed robber had realized she would be the best path to a large payout and had been determined to take her hostage. Patrick's trainer Mike had been with her and was able to distract the guy while Natalie summoned help from the alarm panel. In the ensuing battle, JJ had been shot and battled for his life, and the criminal had been killed.

"Seeing someone die?"

"That." She nodded. "And seeing JJ hurt. Knowing all of it was my fault."

"That's not true at all," he said, shocked she felt that way.

"It is," she insisted. "That guy only died because of me. If I hadn't been here, JJ wouldn't have been shot and the other guy wouldn't have been killed. He had committed a bunch of crimes before he broke in here, but he had never hurt anyone."

"He made the choices that he made," Liam said slowly. "He came here to rob Patrick, thinking it was a big empty house. That was a bad idea on many levels, and he made it worse when he saw you and had the idea to take you with him. You did exactly what JJ had asked you to do, you spent the weekend here, not letting anyone know you were here. Right?"

"Yes," she nodded. "But if I wasn't so flashy and over the top, he probably wouldn't have even known who I was when he saw me. And maybe it was a bad idea to even come here to begin with. But I didn't feel safe in California, and now I don't feel safe here. Plus, I feel guilty. It's a lot to overcome."

"But you're alive," he said. "And JJ is alive. Listen to me carefully, okay? I understand what you're saying about being too recognizable, but this is what our lives have been. For years, it's been trying to get people to look at us, pay attention, and give us jobs. Now we're richer and more famous than we could have ever dreamed, and it's hard to turn it off. Patrick seems to have mastered that here, and I think we can too."

"Is that why you grew that hideous beard?"

"Hey," he said with false hurt. "You don't like it?"

"Hate it," she said.

"I'll shave tomorrow. I did grow it on purpose, because no one recognized me when I had the beard and a hat on," he said. "But it's itchy."

"People don't recognize me as much since I colored my hair," she admitted. "And I started dressing more like Emma and Zoe."

"What I wanted to say," he continued. "Is that you shouldn't be ashamed to be who you are. Yes, you make movies. Yes, you're gorgeous. But you get to have safety and privacy, just like anyone else. Nothing about that night was your fault."

She stared into the fire for a few minutes, and he could see the sheen of tears in her eyes. "I wish it was that easy."

He pulled her towards him so that she rested against his chest and sat with her until she fell asleep. Leaning back against the couch, he decided he could manage sleeping this way if it meant she finally got some rest. Natalie was like a little sister to him, and he was determined to help her get over this trauma and get back to being herself.

Chapter 3

Rex arrived at Jake and Shea's house the next morning, in a small SUV driven by his trainer, Harrison. Holly waited for them on the porch, sipping on her hot coffee and shivering in her jacket, smiling when the car pulled into the driveway. Harrison waved from the driver's seat and parked, assisting the dog out of his seatbelt before coming over to give her a hug. They had dated for a brief blink of time years ago before deciding they were better off as friends, and she had been even more grateful for that decision when she met Jake. Her brother-in-law's PTSD could be debilitating, and she had known instantly that Harrison would be able to help. He specially trained service dogs to assist soldiers exactly like Jake, and he had happily agreed to help.

Rex, a beautiful yellow labrador retriever, sat calmly at Harrisons side as they reunited. He waited for a signal before he trotted over to the grass and relieved himself, returning immediately to his trainer. "Let's get these two introduced again," Harrison said. "I'm excited to see his new home."

Holly led him into the house, where a nervous-looking Jake sat holding the baby. Shea jumped to her feet, then sat back down next to him, looking unsure of herself. "Hey, Harrison," she said. "I don't know what to do."

"Don't stress," he said calmly. "I'm going to re-introduce Jake and Rex and help them get settled. This will be easy since they had weeks of training together at the center. No one needs to act differently than normal, not even Jake. Rex will ignore anything other than Jake and what he's trained to look for. Even when he's sleeping, he'll be aware of anything that could be happening. He'll stay close to Jake and essentially disregard everyone else. Nothing you do will set him off or distract him from the job he's here to do."

"It seems sad," Shea said. "While I'm so grateful to have him for Jake, I worry that he never gets to just be a dog and have fun."

"He can," Harrison explained. "Jake can play catch with him, go for runs, or anything a normal pet would do. It's just that he's going to stick closely with Jake and take his commands from him and have a little less interaction with other dogs than pets might have. Anything that could put him in danger, we discourage."

"My dad has dogs," Jake said. "And some friends do as well."

"As long as you're keeping an eye on the situation, he can be around them, maybe even play. Especially with dogs that you trust," Harrison said. "But don't let him off a leash at a dog park, with animals you don't know. I'm here for a few days to help you adjust, so we'll get through all of this."

Jake reached over and stroked the dog, who was sitting patiently at his feet. "I'm curious to see how all of this works. I wish I didn't need him, but I don't want to feel like my PTSD is keeping me from being a part of my family."

"No shame in needing him," Harrison said confidently. "Seeing the good these dogs are doing for veterans is what keeps me going. I think you'll find a huge difference in your life, for the better."

Jake passed Izzie to his wife, and he, Harrison and Rex headed outside to start their transition. Rex would easily settle in with Jake as his new handler, especially since Jake had some initial training at Harrison's ranch a few months prior. Patrick had made sure they would have plenty of time together, wanting his brother to find peace after years of service. The baby arriving had forced Harrison to suggest they bring Rex once the family was settled back at home, rather than returning from training with Jake. Fortunately, he had also agreed to spend a few days at the Inn in Windsor Peak in case Jake needed any help. Holly was sure that Patrick's generosity had helped fuel that decision, but she was still grateful for all her friend had done for Jake.

"What's on the agenda for today?" Holly asked, dropping into the chair next to Shea.

"Everyone is coming here in a few hours," she said. "We'll start making plans for a fundraiser to rebuild the youth center. And we have a lot of Christmas things to get done."

"I'm a great shopper," Holly offered.

"Perfect, I'll get you a list," Shea said. "Anything to help would be great. School goes right up until Christmas Eve, and the Christmas Festival this weekend will make things even crazier than usual."

"I'm surprised they decided to go ahead with it after what happened to Natalie over the Harvest Festival."

"It's a great boost to our town economy," Shea said. "We get so many tourists, and the way it's set up, people can ski all day and still hit the festival at night. Although now that I said that, I realize we have a problem."

"What's that?"

"The festival was going to be set up at the youth center," Shea said. "It would have been a good boost for them, and kids could be entertained while parents shopped. Now we lost our location."

"That's a big problem," Holly said. "I can't believe no one thought of that last night."

"I know," Shea said. "I imagine the mayor and organizers are scrambling today. Kendra will know more; she and Zoe have a lot to do with the events."

***

"I spoke with the mayor," Ben Burrows announced once they were all settled around the living room hours later. "She was very grateful for our offers to help, especially with the pull that you three will have."

Natalie, Patrick and Liam all nodded, and Holly did her best to ignore Liam. It had gotten harder when he arrived at the door a few minutes earlier, having shaved his beard. Dressed in a flannel and jeans, he could have fit right in with the rest of the town if he wasn't so shockingly gorgeous. His black hair was just a little too long, starting to curl around his neck and ears, and fell just a bit over his forehead, bringing attention to his chocolate-brown eyes. She hadn't realized he had a dimple in his chin, but it was now out on full display, as was one on his left cheek. It was easy to see why he made his living on a movie screen, and hard to remind herself to stay away.

"The first issue is the Christmas Festival next weekend," Ben continued. "They have decided to move it to the elementary school. They said they can figure out the logistics for that, so one less thing for us to worry about. Kendra, I'm sure you'll be involved, so if you need help, just say the word."

"Thanks," Kendra said. "JJ, how bad is the youth center?"

"The fire did a lot of damage," he shared. "But it isn't a total loss. It damaged all the office space, and some of the rooms they use to do smaller classes or homework time. The gym, track, and exercise room will be salvageable. Most of the equipment will need to be replaced, just because of water damage."

"How long will it all take?" Patrick asked.

"Months, most likely," Jake said. "That's a bigger job than I could take on, but I can't see it happening fast."

"That's terrible," Shea said. "So many of the students depend on that space for a safe place to go, or for a meal."

"Is there another space in town that could be used in the meantime?" Holly asked, surprising even herself. "Maybe an empty building that could be repurposed?"

"That's a thought," Ben nodded. "There isn't anything big enough on Main Street that I can think of."

"No," Kendra agreed. "We took over the empty space next to the Palace, but even that would have been too small."

Holly knew that Kendra, the owner of the local restaurant Windsor Palace, had recently expanded into a catering and event space with Zoe. The two had been working together for years, with Zoe heading up the kitchen while Kendra managed the business. The two women had wanted to expand into a partnership on a new venture, and Palace Plates was born. From what Holly had heard, things had been going well for them so far. Shea had reportedly already signed them up for a cooking class dedicated to holiday meals that she promised would be more fun than work, and Holly was excited about it.

"Maybe you could ask Julie?" Shea suggested, referring to Kendra's friend who was a local realtor. "She may know of something that we aren't aware of."

"I'll do that," Kendra nodded, pulling out her phone.

"While we're waiting for her to get back to us, a few reminders," Stella said. "I know the next few weeks will be busy, and we have lots of plans coming up. On Wednesday the girls are going to the Christmas candle making event that Zoe is organizing at Palace Plates. We also have cookie decorating, breakfast with Santa, and a million other things. Oh, and you young ones have Christmas Karaoke at the Palace. Ben and I will manage just fine with the babies and Calle, we'll have Charlie there to help as well."

"The four of them together can be a lot," Kendra said. "Maybe Shea and I should—"

"Enjoy a night out with your husband and friends? Yes." Stella had a look on her face that said she meant business, and Holly had to hold in a laugh at how quickly Kendra and Shea gave in.

"Julie said she might have an option," Kendra announced. "She asked if anyone could come meet her right now to see it. We can't go, the baby needs to eat, and Calle has a very detailed schedule for family pizza night."

"Izzie is going to need to be fed as well, and Charlie has hockey practice," Shea said. "That takes Jake and I out."

"Ben and I have dinner plans with some friends," Stella said.

"I can go," Liam offered. "I've got nothing happening."

"Holly, can you go with him? You know your way around and you've met Julie a few times," Shea asked. "That would be a huge help."

Realizing her sister was trying to make sure that Patrick and Emma wouldn't have to leave Natalie alone, she nodded reluctantly. This had not been on her bingo card for the holiday, but she would do just about anything for Shea. Even if it meant spending an hour alone with the grump who had ruined her favorite sweater.

Chapter 4

"I had no idea I was wandering into Christmas wonderland when I agreed to come here," Liam griped as they got into the borrowed car. "I thought it would be a quiet couple of weeks spent skiing and helping Natalie."

"Too much to ask that you also help out the town that Patrick loves?" Holly snapped her seatbelt in as she fired the words at him, and he flinched.

"Ouch," he said. "You make me sound horrible."

"I don't make you sound anything."

"You think I'm a jerk?"

"Absolutely," she said, starting the car and cranking the heat to high. "Especially now that you're complaining about some holiday fun."

"I've just never been a big fan of Christmas," he explained. "It wasn't like this growing up."

"What was it like?" She pulled out of the driveway onto the road that would wind down the mountain towards town, driving far slower than he would have if he had the keys.

"My parents usually worked," he answered. "We didn't do much."

"Do you have siblings? And what do you mean, worked? On Christmas?"

"No to the siblings. And yes." He nodded. "My mom is a nurse. Or was a nurse. My dad was a firefighter. They both retired a few years ago. They got holiday pay to work, and they couldn't turn that down."

"And you'd just be home, alone?" She sounded horrified, and he realized this was not at all something he had planned to share.

"It's really not a big deal," he said.

"Where are your parents now? Why aren't you spending the holidays with them?"

"They are spending the winter in Florida," he answered. "Natalie needed me here. And I have to admit, snow wins over sand every time, so it wasn't a hard push to get me here."

"You must have had some Christmas traditions," she pushed. "Movies? Hot cocoa? Decorating a tree?"

"Nope," he said. "I would usually have a full stocking and some gifts when I woke up, and then I would wait until one of them got home. It really wasn't a big deal."

"I feel like we need to fix this," she said. "No wonder you're such a grinch. You need some Christmas magic in your life."

"Please don't," he said. "That sounds like the last thing I need."

She pulled into a driveway and parked before looking at him again. "We'll see about that," she said, breaking eye contact as she turned to get out of the car. Suddenly, the idea of spending more time with her and allowing her to share her holiday spirit didn't sound so terrible.

A second car pulled into the driveway, a woman behind the wheel. "That's Julie, the real estate agent," Holly said, opening her door.

Julie got out and hugged Holly before shaking his hand, barely acknowledging who he was. "This is it," she said, pointing to the buildings in front of them. "This has been empty for a while. The barn is huge, and there is a second building that was used for functions. It has a full kitchen, plenty of tables already there, and bathrooms. The barn is big enough to bring in some basketball hoops or whatever else they need. It's heated too, so the cold isn't an issue."

"But this is a home," he said, glancing over at the large farmhouse that the realtor hadn't acknowledged.

"It was," she said. "It's fully furnished, being sold as is. The owner lost his wife and decided to move south a year ago, and it's been empty ever since. It's expensive, so a hard sell. But it's an easy walk from the school, and on the bus route. I thought I could talk to him, see if he could donate it as long as the utilities were covered while it's in use."

He surveyed the property, the three buildings surrounded by what he presumed was grass under the snow. Not another person or house was in sight, but he could see the school they had passed on their drive, and the steeple of the church that was in town. "How much?"

"For the utilities? I'm not sure," Julie said.

"No, for the property," he said. "I'll take it. See if the guy is willing to close immediately if we do a cash transaction. If it would take a week or two, ask him if we can have access to it immediately if I put the full amount into escrow."

"What?" Holly was staring at him, mouth agape.

"Ditto," Julie laughed. "I haven't even told you the price."

He looked at the ground for a moment and shrugged, unsure of how to act in this moment. Arrogant actor? Humble millionaire? Himself? "It's not an issue."

"Why don't I make an offer that I think he'll accept, and we can go from there," Julie said. She wrote something down in her small notebook and held it up for only him to see. "Will that work?"

"If you think so," he said. "But I'm willing to go higher if need be. The most important thing is that it be done as quickly as possible so that the kids can start coming here. Oh, and one more thing."

"Yes?" Julie looked at him expectantly, but he looked at Holly as he spoke.

"No one needs to know that I bought this," he said. "This can stay between the three of us for now."

"Why? It's so incredible of you to buy this and let the youth center use it," Julie asked. Holly stayed quiet, but he could see the same question in her eyes.

"It's not a big deal, and I don't want Patrick and Natalie to be hurt that I'm doing this without them," he said. "Plus, I need an investment property. My manager has been telling me that for years." It was a fib, but they didn't need to know that he already owned homes in California, New York and London, as well as land in some other areas.

"I don't mind," Julie said with a smile. "This will be my biggest sale of the year if we can get it done, so I'm happy to keep my mouth shut."

"Is this putting you in a weird place with Shea?" he asked Holly, seeing the conflict on her face.

"A little bit," she admitted. "But it's for a good cause, so I can manage."

"We can tell them once the youth center is repaired," he told her.

"We won't be here when that's done," she reminded him.

"True," he said. "But I'll come back and let Patrick know. Get the ball rolling on some renovations so that I can use this as a ski house. Or a quiet place to relax."

"A multi-million-dollar place to relax." Holly laughed. "I think they have spas for that."

"But spas don't have my best friend down the street, and no paparazzi," he said with a smile.

"I'm going to head back to town to write this up and get it over to him immediately," Julie said. "I can call you when I have an answer."

He looked at Holly again. "Do you mind giving her your number?" Julie looked briefly insulted and he felt bad. "It's not personal. I have to change my number constantly when it finds its way into the public's hands, or when a reporter won't stop calling. It's not that I don't trust you, but I could very well have to change it later today. It happens that fast."

She nodded, and the two women exchanged numbers before Julie got in the car and drove away. Holly studied him for a moment before looking back at the property. "Want to see what you just bought?"

"Sure," he said with a laugh. "Probably should have done that first."

Holly held up a key ring and smiled at him. "Julie thought the same, but she was happy to run off with your offer and leave me the keys."

They spent the next hour walking through the buildings, noting the massive space that the former owners had used as a wedding venue. The home had been converted into a bed and breakfast and would need updating, but the industrial kitchen was perfect for now. The house could be used as office space and overflow to make the kids meals, so every bit of the two outer buildings could hold activities.

"I think they can make some small changes and have this ready to go this week," he said to Holly after they had finished walking through everything.

"Absolutely." She nodded. "Maybe some Christmas decorations. We could even have the kids come one afternoon to help with that."

"I don't think it needs that," he argued. "Seems like a waste."

"A waste to make the space festive for the kids? They're probably bouncing off the walls in excitement over the holiday," she said. Her gaze softened as she looked at him. "And maybe some of them don't have a tree at home to decorate or anyone to make garland with."

"Why would you make your own garland?"

"Oh, we have some work to do. I'm going to make it my personal mission to share my love for Christmas with you," she promised. "I'll turn you from a grinch to a Griswold."

"Is this the right time to tell you I have no idea what a Griswold is?"

She stared at him in disbelief for a long moment and then laughed. "Okay, this might be more fun than I thought. Let's go, coffee boy. We have a lot to do."

Chapter 5

Holly studied the man next to her from the corner of her eye as she drove. He was texting rapidly on his phone before sticking it in his pocket, glancing over at her as he did. She quickly looked at the road, not wanting him to know she had been looking. He was by far the most attractive man she had ever seen, other than Patrick perhaps. But Patrick was like family to her and clearly in love with Emma, so she didn't notice his looks as much anymore. Liam, on the other hand, had a reputation as a playboy. Every awards show and movie premiere, he had a different woman on his arm. A woman who almost always looked like a model, knowing how to pose and be caught just right on camera.

Unlike what he was used to in California, Holly was dressed in leggings, a thermal shirt and a sweater, and warm boots. Her life didn't call for slinky dresses and sky-high heels, and she rarely wore makeup or styled her hair. Everything about their lives was opposite, she decided. The tingling she felt around him was simply because he was nice to look at, and the surprising generosity he exhibited showed he did have a heart in there. Somewhere.

A text popped up on the screen in the car, where the map from her phone was displayed. She clicked on it to be read out loud to both of them and smiled when the automated voice told them that the seller had accepted his offer.

"Do you mind if we swing by Dan's office?" he asked. "I'd like him to look at the paperwork before I sign."

"You might own that house today?"

"Looks that way," he said. "I'm waiving inspections, although I'll have them done myself for the kid's safety. It will just speed things along if I do everything later."

"But you could be paying more than you should be," she pointed out.

He shrugged and looked out the window. "It's just money," he said finally. "I can't take it with me. And there's plenty more to make."

She laughed quickly, then realized he was being serious. "That must be weird," she ventured. "To know your next job will equal the annual budget of a small country."

"What do you do for work?" he asked, turning towards her again and making the space feel smaller somehow.

"I'm a nurse," she answered.

"Like my mom," he said. "Do you like it?"

"I do," she said with a nod. "It's hard some days, but it's satisfying."

"Would you do it no matter what?"

"Probably," she answered.

"That's how I feel about acting," he said. "It's amazing that I finally made it, after a long struggle. But even if I hadn't, if I was doing off-off-Broadway, or an indie film for nothing, I would still be doing it. It's in my blood."

"I'm guessing success makes it a little easier, though," she said.

"I spent a lot of years really roughing it. I slept on people's couches; I worked all sorts of crazy jobs to have money for food. New York and Los Angeles are not cheap to live in, and it was a daily struggle. One time I made one peanut butter and jelly sandwich last for three days, because I couldn't afford anything else," he said. "I didn't have my own place to live until my first movie, and there were times where I slept in my car. So, yeah, I'd say making money is better."

"Unfortunately, no one is offering me millions to care for their loved one," she said drolly. "But I'd happily take it if they did."

"We have nurses on set," he said. "If you're ever interested, let me know."

"Thanks. I live in Nevada right now, but I'm on a travel assignment," she said.

"What does that mean?"

"I take nursing assignments, traveling to the location and staying there for the duration of the contract," she explained. "It's allowed me to go all around the country, which is amazing."

"Kind of like acting," he said. "I have been to so many places I never thought I would go. I don't get to see a lot of them, especially now, but it's nice to at least have a brief glance."

They pulled into the small parking lot behind the building where Dan's law office was. "Why can't you see them?" she asked as they both climbed out of the SUV. "I try to get out as much as possible when I'm in a new place. I think when I get tired of exploring, I'll have to pick my favorite place and settle down. It will be a good indicator that I'm done traveling."

"I have a visibility problem," he said. "It's rare that I can be somewhere and walk down the street like this."

"Oh, I didn't think of that. It must be easier here, since everyone already knows Patrick."

He held the door open, waving for her to go ahead of him. "It's a lot easier than almost anywhere else," he said. "New York, Los Angeles, and Paris are the three where I can be out and ignored. People are too cool to swarm me there. Anywhere else, I can usually count on it."

"I guess you can add Windsor Peak to that list of safe places," she said.

He smiled at her, causing those butterflies to start up again. "I guess so."

Holly watched as he signed paperwork with Dan before he turned back to her. "Want to get some lunch? Dan, can you join us?"

"I can't," Dan said, holding up the papers. "You just gave me a bunch of work to do. But I'll take a rain check."

"Let me know when it's all set, and I'll have the money guy make the transfer. And thanks for agreeing to keep this between us for now. We'll see you later," Liam said. He opened the door and gestured for Holly to walk through. "Where to?"

"Windsor Peak Palace is Kendra's restaurant, where Zoe works," Holly answered. "Or if you want something more casual, Slice Girls has pizza and the bakery has sandwiches and salads."

"Hey." A voice from behind them had Liam stiffening even as Holly turned in recognition. Liam had obviously thought it was a fan about to interrupt them, but she knew the voice.

"Harrison," she said warmly, hugging him. "How's it going?"

"It's been great," he said. "I love this town, I need to come back for a longer visit. I was going to call you and say goodbye, I'm about to head to the airport."

"Oh, thank you so much for coming out. Next time we'll have more of a chance to hang out," she promised. "Text me when you get home safe."

"Will do," he said, hugging her one more time before heading into the bakery.

"If you're done flirting, can we get some lunch?" Liam's voice broke through her spell as she watched Harrison walk away. She felt bad that she hadn't been able to spend much time with him, but he had been busy with Jake and Rex for the few days he was in town.

"Flirting? I can do much better than that," she said dryly. "That was Harrison, he's the trainer who brought the service dog up for Jake."

"Sorry, I get cranky when I'm hungry," he said. "Let's go to the Palace, the last time I was here I had an unbelievable meal there."

"Perfect, that will give us time to make a list," she said. She crossed the street, seeing heads swivel when they recognized the man she was with, but no one approached them.

"List of what?"

"Christmas activities," she answered. "And things the property needs for the holidays."

He opened the door and waved for her to go first. "I still don't think it's necessary. It's two weeks until Christmas, there's no reason to waste the time decorating."

"Waste time?" She stared at him in horror. "For some kids, the only Christmas trees they'll see are the ones at school or in town. Or in this case, at the youth center. The kids like you, who don't have it at home."

He looked confused as he accepted a menu from a waitress, who was openly staring at him with starstruck eyes. He took a moment to smile at her, then turned back to Holly. "Why don't they have one at home?"

"They're expensive," she said. "I know Shea talks about how some of her students never get gifts, and she always feels bad when they come back from break and some kids got a ton and others nothing. She works her butt off to make sure everyone has at least one gift each year, but the decorations are out of her control."

"Where does she get the gifts?"

"The church does a giving tree, and a lot of the local businesses will contribute. The ski resort always does a donation box, and they'll run specials where people can trade donations for a day on the slopes," she said. "This little town looks out for its own."

"Must be amazing to be a part of it," he mused. "Okay, I'll get some trees, and you can help me decorate. Happy?"

"Not even close," she said. She took out her phone and wrote in her notes app as she talked. "We need to make gingerbread houses. Go caroling. Volunteer for a local cause. Build a snowman. Make cookies. What am I missing?"

"Dress up as Santa Claus and deliver all the presents with my reindeer?"

She pointed a finger at him, scowling. "You're not taking this seriously."

"Absolutely not," he said, shaking his head. "I told you; I don't do Christmas. If you want to put up a few trees or toss some tinsel up, have at it."

"And what will you be doing?"

"What I came for," he said with a shrug. "Help Natalie."

"By doing what, exactly? Do you think sitting and staring at her is going to help?"

"No, but—"

"Maybe the best thing for her would be to engage in festive activities," she pushed on. "We could do all of this with her, make her feel safe and begin to feel happy again. You could do that for her, *we* could do that for her."

"Why are you so involved? This was supposed to be your holiday time with your sister and your new niece. Why the insistence to do all this for Natalie?"

"I've seen some dark things in nursing," she told him. "And I've gone to therapy, been able to move past it. But I've had coworkers who couldn't, who were just haunted by the accidents or injuries they have seen. Not to mention, I've gotten to know

Jake well over the last year, and Shea has shared a lot of what he goes through with his PTSD. I don't want Natalie to have to go through that. She didn't sign up for this, it happened to her. That's terrible."

He stared at her until the waitress returned to take their order and had to clear her throat to get his attention. Finally, he nodded. "You're on," he said. "I'll work with you to help her. But I won't be festive."

"We'll just see about that."

Chapter 6

Two days passed, which were spent rattling around in Patrick's sprawling farmhouse with Natalie. Patrick and Emma had been busy, Christmas shopping and doing some volunteer work at the animal shelter, but Liam had exactly nothing going on. He worked out with Patrick's trainer, Mike, who tried to get Natalie to exercise with them. He soaked in the hot tub, alone because Nat wouldn't join him there either. When he tried to broach the subject of a horseback ride, she shot him down before he could even ask the question. By the end of the second day, he was going stir crazy and was relieved when Dan pulled into the driveway.

"Hey," he said, pulling the door open. "What's up?"

"You alone?" Dan asked, scraping the ice off his shoes before stepping inside.

"Nat is here, but she's curled up in the theater watching a movie," he said.

"Then I can officially tell you that you're now a homeowner in Windsor Peak," Dan said. He produced a legal-size envelope from the messenger bag he had and handed it over. "Keys are in there, and all the paperwork."

Liam fiddled with the seal, unsure of himself yet again. Dan had been his lawyer for years, and they had hung out some through Patrick. He was a nice guy and a solid person on his team, but they didn't know each other well. It was a weird space between friendship and a work relationship, and he never knew what to do. Invite him to have a beer? Shake his hand and send him along? Both felt awkward and wrong, and he hated that he couldn't just relax.

"Patrick and Emma should be back soon," he finally said. "Do you want to grab a beer and wait?"

"Nah." Dan waved his hand. "You'd have to explain why I'm here, and I don't want to give up your secrets. Plus, Kendra and the kids are waiting for me. We have to decorate the tree still."

"I thought you all did that the day after Thanksgiving?"

"We get them that day," Dan explained. "But things have been hectic for Kendra. The holiday festival is next weekend, and she's been out straight. But she promised that she would make the time tonight, so I can't be the reason why we're not doing it."

"Got it. Thanks for this," Liam said. "I'll see you around."

"Don't feel like you have to keep that a secret," Dan advised him. "Patrick will be thrilled."

"I know," he said, shrugging. "I just don't want to be the guy who swoops into town and solves problems with money, you know?"

"I do." Dan nodded. "But you could also be the guy who saves everything with hard work, and some money. Get in there; make it ready for the kids. It will be good to have a project, and I bet Natalie could use something to do."

"Exactly my plan," he said. "Speaking of, do you happen to have Holly's number?"

Dan cocked an eyebrow but shook his head. "I don't, sorry. But I can text Shea and get it if you want?"

"Thanks," he said, feeling weird again. It was easy to ask Dan to handle professional things, but personal issues were more complicated.

"I'll send it to you when she forwards it," Dan promised, heading for the door. "Congrats on the house."

Liam watched as Dan left, and then headed for the stairs to the lower level, where Patrick's massive theater room was. Natalie was curled up in a recliner, a blanket covering most of her. She looked tiny and young, and even the comedy on the screen wasn't bringing a smile to her face.

"Hey," he said, plopping down next to her. "I want to show you something. Let's go for a ride."

"No thanks," she said. "I'm in the middle of a movie."

"You've seen this at least ten times," he argued. "Please? I think you'll like it."

"Nothing in the public, right?"

"No one but us," he said. "And maybe Holly, if I get her number."

Interest bloomed on her face for the first time since he had arrived. "Oh, is that a thing?"

"No, it's not a thing. I just happen to know that she wants to help with this project."

"She's very pretty," Natalie said, her voice teasing. "Not your usual type, though."

"What does that mean?"

"You usually go for the supermodels. The girls with extensions, fake lashes, big lips and bigger—"

"I get what you're saying," he interrupted her. "But that's not all I date."

"Isn't it? Holly is gorgeous, but she doesn't seem to wear much makeup, and she's usually dressed for comfort, not to impress," Natalie said. "But I bet if she went all out, she'd be prettier than anyone you've ever dated."

"It's not just about looks, Nat."

"It shouldn't be," she said as she nodded. "But you have a way of staying in the shallow waters. Maybe it's time you found someone like her, who's as pretty on the inside as she is on the outside. And let yourself be open to the possibility when you are around someone like that."

"I will try, but only if you come with me," he tried.

Natalie narrowed her eyes at him, assessing. "One condition."

"Name it."

"Ask her on a date," she challenged.

"Who?"

"Holly," she said, rolling her eyes. "You knew who I was talking about."

"She doesn't want to date me," he argued.

"How do you know?"

"I just do. A woman like that wants someone who's secure and leads a normal life. Not me."

"Did she say that?"

"She doesn't need to," he said. "It happens every time. Remember my girlfriend when we started the first movie? I thought I was going to marry her. And she dropped me once the spotlight was on us."

"That's one person," she said. "That doesn't mean everyone feels the same."

He considered her again, seeing the bags under her eyes and how pale she looked. The last few weeks had put a strain on her, and no one had been able to pull her out of it. According to Patrick, they had tried being delicate with her, then tried tough love. They had her seeing a therapist, and she had even tried a hypnotist. Nothing had made her feel better about the trauma she had been through.

"Deal," he said. The one date might mean that Natalie would leave the house with him and get involved in his project. And maybe, as Holly had suggested, this was just what Nat needed.

***

He drove the short distance to the new property, keeping half an eye on Natalie to make sure she didn't get out of the car and run back. She was bundled into a sweater, heavy coat and boots, and had a ski cap on her head. "Warm enough?" he asked her, reaching for the controls.

"I'm fine," she said. "Where are we going?"

He shook his head, returning both hands to the wheel. "We're almost there, and then I'll tell you."

She looked confused when he turned away from the small downtown area, and her eyes widened as they pulled in the long driveway. The house was a sprawling rustic farmhouse, the warm pine color of the wood standing out against the mountains behind it. The main building branched off on either side, causing the house to form a C-shape, with the exterior of the sides done in a dark blue to blend with the sky and mountain. The previous owner had broken the wings from the main house into small private apartments when converting to a bed and breakfast, so the owner and a caretaker could live in privacy. There were also several small cottages set back on the property that were rented out for larger groups. In the distance, they could see the large buildings that housed the barn and the event space, separated by walking paths and a small pond.

"What is this?" she asked, unbuckling her seatbelt.

"Hopefully the new youth center," he answered. "At least until they can rebuild the original one."

A second car pulled in, and he saw Holly behind the wheel. She waved before opening her door, smiling at both of them. "Hey, Nat," she said, hugging the other woman. "I'm so glad to see you."

"You too," Nat said. "Did you know about this?"

"I did." She nodded and smiled at them. Liam gestured towards the house, and they all started walking as she continued to talk. "He swore me to secrecy, but I saw it the other day. It's going to be amazing when we're done."

"What are you thinking?"

"First, we need to get some holiday decorations in here," Holly said. "In addition to getting some activities in place for the kids. I talked to Shea, and she said they can always make the event space work, and just have the kids focus on doing homework and small crafts or games at the tables. But the kids have energy to burn after school, and I think a space where they can run it off is important."

"Agreed," Liam said. "I asked my assistant to look into how fast we can get some things set up in the barn. He thinks it would be easier to rent things and have them removed when the new building is ready, but I told him whatever is faster. At least half a basketball court, plus open space for other games. Jump rope, dancing, anything that will get them moving."

"You have plenty of space for outdoor activities as well," Holly pointed out. "Assuming the kids have the right gear."

"What would they need?" Natalie asked.

"Snow pants, boots, hats, warm jackets, and gloves," Holly ticked off on her fingers.

"They don't have that already?" Natalie looked horrified. "It's freezing here."

"Some of them do, but maybe don't wear it all to school," Holly said. "According to Shea, others don't. She helps organize a drive every year for most of it and tries to make sure every kid has the basics. But there's always a few who are too proud, and they don't come. Then, they show up for school wearing just a sweatshirt when it's below twenty degrees."

"Unacceptable," Natalie said. "I'll get my assistant working on this."

"Better yet," Holly said, "we could go shopping."

Liam watched as the emotions flickered across Natalie's face. She had been reluctant to leave Patrick's home for any reason over the last few weeks, since the shooting. The one time Patrick said he convinced her to go to dinner, she ran from the restaurant in a panic and didn't get out of bed for days. The furthest she had gone was to the Burrows family homes, and even that took persuasion. Going to a big store and shop would be a huge step, and he was surprised to see that she was even considering it. He was even more shocked when she nodded. "Okay, that will get them supplies faster. Let's do it."

Chapter 7

Holly saw the spark of life in Natalie's eye at the thought of helping and couldn't help but seize it. She glanced at Liam and saw him nod slightly behind his friend's back, and she linked her arm with Natalie. "Let's check out the property and make a list of what we might need," she said. "Then we can hit the store. Is there anything we can do to make it more comfortable for you?"

"Maybe online would be a better idea," Natalie whispered.

"I can ask them to close," Liam said quickly. "So that we would be the only people there. Or we could go in right after they close, so they don't have to kick other people out."

"That might work," Holly said encouragingly. "Let me text Shea and ask her the best place to go, and we can call."

Liam pulled out his phone as well, sending a text before sticking the phone in his pocket again. "Let's start at the barn," he suggested, pointing in the direction. "Then we can look at the house when we come back this way."

The three of them followed the narrowly shoveled path to the furthest building, which was a wide-open space. They all made suggestions that were helpful, pointing out how different areas could be set up. Crossing to the event space, Holly considered all the tables they could use in different ways for crafting and schoolwork. They discussed the dance floor, and whether it would need to be removed, but Natalie suggested it be moved to a different area to create a small dance studio. The room was too wide open for kids to be productive on schoolwork, they all felt it needed to be divided up somehow and that quiet study areas in the main house would be ideal. When they followed Liam to the farmhouse and entered the first apartment, she smiled. "This is adorable," she said. "This was for a caretaker?"

"Yes." Liam nodded. "Julie said that the house was used as a bed and breakfast, so the apartment allowed the caretaker a bit of privacy. The other one is identical to this, and the owner and his wife lived there."

"Will you live in the main house?" Holly asked, curious of his plans.

"Not right now," he said. "I was thinking the youth center could use it for office space, or if they need to have a nurse out here. Plus, we just saw they need quiet reading rooms for the kids who wouldn't be able to focus in that noise."

"That's very generous of you," she said. "But I don't think it's necessary to give up all of this."

"Maybe I could stay in one of the apartments," he said. "I'd want to have the main house renovated anyway. I'll give it some thought."

They walked quickly through the house before heading out to the cars. "Natalie, why don't you ride with me," she suggested quickly. If her new friend had second thoughts about the shopping trip, she wouldn't put it past Liam to go easy on her and bring her back to Patrick's house. "I have the address from Shea for a store that will have a good supply. Why don't you follow us there?"

"Did Shea mention if the store was open?" Natalie hesitated before opening her car door, clearly torn.

"They are due to close at six," Holly answered. "The manager is someone Shea knows, so she called over and they would be more than happy to stay open for you to shop."

"Okay," Natalie said, looking anything but that.

"I'll follow," Liam said, ducking into the driver's seat of the other car.

As Holly pulled carefully out of the driveway, she glanced over to see Natalie gripping the handle on the car door. "How long have you known Liam and Patrick?"

"Years," Natalie replied. "I did a few small movies before we all were cast in the series, but nothing really took. I was always pretty typecast as a ditzy side character, wearing too little clothing and not enough brain cells. When I got this role, I was thrilled. Getting to play a smart, strong woman who can take care of herself was a huge change, and I am proud to represent that image to little girls everywhere. Then meeting the guys made it even better. We've been our own little dysfunctional but supportive family."

"That's so nice," Holly said, smiling encouragingly at her. "They seem like great guys."

"They are," Natalie said with a smile. "Zane is a little wild, but Liam seems to be growing up finally. Patrick is a good influence on them."

"It's great to see him so happy with Emma."

"Yes, they are great together," Natalie nodded. "I also couldn't help but notice that Liam is quite taken with you."

"Me?" Holly laughed, shock rippling through her. "No chance. He's Liam Dorsey. He wouldn't be interested in me."

"You're right," Nat said. "He definitely doesn't like intelligent, beautiful, successful, confident, nice women."

Holly laughed, her dismay at Natalie's first statement washed away with the second. "I don't think that's how he sees me."

"You'd be surprised. Liam is a mystery, even to me sometimes. He comes off as cocky and arrogant, but there's a much deeper person behind that," Nat said. "I see glimpses of it once in a while, when he looks a little lost and like he's acting to be so confident. I'd love to see who he is with his walls down. Maybe you can get him there."

Holly pulled into the parking spot in front of the store, next to a pickup truck that was still running. "I don't think we'll be here long enough to have that happen," she said to Natalie. "But maybe some Christmas spirit will do him good."

The driver's door of the pickup truck opened, and Nat gasped as the man climbed out. "Did you know Mike was coming?"

"Who's Mike?"

"He's Patrick's friend. His trainer, I mean. Or both."

"Okay," Holly said slowly. "Why are we freaking out? Oh, he's nice to look at, isn't he? And is he really that big or am I imagining it?"

"He's that big, and that delicious," Natalie said softly. "He's also the one who saved my life."

"Oh," Holly said. "Are you okay? You've seen him since, right?"

"Yes, he comes every day." Natalie studied the man who was standing patiently waiting for them outside the car. "Tries to get me to work out with them and tries to talk to me. But he's always been terrible at that, I think I make him nervous."

Holly laughed. "You think? You make me nervous, and I'm a woman. Come on, let's go inside."

Liam and Mike were shaking hands as the two women climbed out of the car, and Mike quickly walked to Natalie's side, talking to her quietly. Holly watched as she nodded, and then slipped her hand into his arm. The man towered over the tiny woman, and his entire presence showed how protective he was of her. Liam was also watching them but turned to meet her eyes and smile. "Thanks for giving her some girl time," he said. "Patrick couldn't come, so he asked Mike to run down to give her some extra support."

They all walked into the empty store together, the manager fawning over both Natalie and Liam equally before encouraging them to pick out what they wanted and offering to deliver it the next day. Natalie nodded, telling the other three that she was picking up the tab and to leave nothing behind. Holly grabbed a Santa hat from a display and arranged it on Liam's head, smiling up at him. "This will be fun."

Liam shocked her by leaning down to kiss her quickly on the cheek, winking at her after he did. The butterflies that had been mildly flying in her stomach kicked into high gear, and she felt a blush spreading across her cheeks. The geeky teenager who still lived inside her wanted to grab the cheek and shriek that she would never wash it again, but she managed to somehow hold it together.

***

"Shea texted me when we were shopping," Holly told Liam as they drove back to Windsor Peak. "She said everyone is going to their house for dinner to talk about the festival and fundraising. But I can drop you off at Patrick's if you'd rather."

"No, that sounds perfect," he said. He was distracted, looking at his phone, and she felt a hint of disappointment surge through her. For a minute, when they were shopping, she felt like she was seeing the true Liam, the one Natalie mentioned. But now, he seemed to have shut down again, focused on his phone and having lost his smile.

"Is there something wrong?"

He frowned, pulling his attention back to her. "No, why would you say that?"

"You just seem to have something intense happening there," she said, pointing at his phone.

"Oh, my agent is pushing me to do some things I don't want to do," he said. "I need a break and I told him that, but he keeps asking me anyway. And my manager is texting me nonstop about the house and some other stuff I have to deal with."

"Sorry, I wasn't thinking," she said. "I have the kind of job that when I leave, I get to forget about it. I guess you never really get to turn it off."

"No, and I have people who work for me that rely on me being responsive," he said. "As much as I seem like a guy who doesn't care, I do. I don't want to go silent on them, or not ask my assistant to do things, because it freaks them out. My assistant told me once he would rather I ask him to do something really stupid, just so he knows he has job security."

"What you're saying is that some of this reliance on other people is for their sake?"

He laughed and nodded. "I guess when you put it like that, yes."

She pulled in the driveway, Natalie and Mike just behind her. The four of them piled into the front door, pulling off jackets and boots before joining everyone in the kitchen. Holly found herself in the doorway, next to Liam, when her sister's eyes took them in.

Shea broke into a giant smile and pointed at them, looking so happy with herself that Holly felt instant dread. "You two are under the mistletoe," Shea called to them. "It's seven years of bad luck if you don't kiss."

"I don't think that's right," Jake laughed.

"Not really worth the risk," Liam murmured as everyone else's attention moved on to discussing the myth. He leaned closer to her, so she could smell the scent that had been teasing her nose all day. A mix of oranges and some kind of tree, she decided, and whatever it was made her feel almost intoxicated. Liam's eyes met hers as he slowly closed the gap, and she suddenly found it hard to breathe. His mouth was less than an inch from hers, his warm breath causing her to lick her own lips, when he spoke again. "May I?"

She felt her head nod in the slightest, so caught up in the moment she couldn't even form words. The idea that her lips could ache to be kissed had never occurred to her, but that was what she was feeling at this moment.

He hovered there, sharing the air she breathed, before suddenly detouring and kissing just to the side of her lips. "I'm not a fan of an audience, at least for a first kiss," he said quietly. "I'll keep my eye out for some private mistletoe."

Chapter 8

Liam punched the pillow again, flipping over and groaning when he saw another hour had passed and he hadn't been able to fall asleep. The night had been fine, he had enjoyed talking to Jake about his new service dog, Rex. Learning about the ways the dog helped with his PTSD had been eye opening, he could tell that Jake was more relaxed. The dog had never left his side, and when Stella had dropped a tray, the dog instantly put his head on Jake's leg, as if sensing the impact the sudden noise had on him.

Unfortunately, Liam had no such comfort, and was feeling unsettled for all the wrong reasons, although nothing as significant as what his friend had gone through. Despite his best efforts to ignore the cause, his subconscious would not let him off that easy. The only thing that could offer him comfort right now was a certain woman, who was wrong for him in so many ways. Even the idea of running to New York for a few nights to ease the restlessness wasn't catching on, and it wasn't just the thought of leaving when Natalie needed him. Holly had captured his interest, and it was such a bad idea on so many levels that he knew he couldn't do anything about it.

Women flocked to him constantly and wanted to be seen on his arm, but they never wanted to actually know the man inside. He and Zane had made a habit out of finding a date for the night, but nothing lasted longer than that. Patrick settling down had been inevitable, he had been born to be in a relationship. But Liam hadn't been in a relationship since becoming famous, and the thought of it was unsettling. Holly was the first woman he had ever talked to who he felt cared more about who he was on the inside his heart than what was in his bank or what he looked like on the outside. He did not intimidate her, and acted as though he was a normal person, calling him out on his bad behavior and seemingly having high expectations of him. He didn't know how to deal with a woman like that.

Giving up on sleep, he headed downstairs to find a bottle of whiskey, or anything that would help him turn off his brain. He was startled at the bottom of the stairs to find Natalie curled up on a couch by a roaring fire, a glass of wine in front of her.

"Hey," he said softly, not wanting to scare her. "Can't sleep?"

"I don't do much of that anymore," she said. "Especially not at night."

"Nat—"

"Please," she said, holding up a hand. "Don't start with me right now. I'm doing everything I can to get better, and I just can't handle talking about it for one more second."

"Okay," he said. He caught sight of the wine bottle next to her and grabbed a glass from Patrick's sidebar, filling it from the bottle before settling onto the couch across from her. "What should we talk about instead?"

"Why are you awake?"

"I can't sleep," he said.

"Why?"

"No idea," he said. "I've always been a bad sleeper. You know that."

They sat in silence for a few minutes, both watching the flames flicker. Emma had hung stockings up over the fireplace for them all, and he couldn't help but smile at them. "What's that about?" Natalie demanded, studying him.

"What?"

"The smile," she said.

"I was just thinking how lucky I am that I got cast with you guys," he said. "Our stockings there made me think about what an odd little family we've become."

Natalie's face softened as she met his eyes. "I really do appreciate you coming here," she said. "I know you'd probably rather be on a beach somewhere picking up random women."

"No place I'd rather be," he said, realizing it was the truth.

"Holly seems great," Natalie said, sipping her wine and watching him over the rim.

"She's nice," he said guardedly.

"Pretty too," she said.

"You know it's not about looks," he argued.

She almost spit out her wine when she laughed, the sound seeming to surprise her. He couldn't help but laugh along, and before he knew it, they were both unable to stop. When they finally did, she wiped her eyes before speaking again. "Wow, that felt good. I haven't laughed in a long time."

"I'm glad you can laugh at my expense," he said, pretending to be hurt. She laughed again, and he was thrilled to get the reaction he had hoped for.

"You have dated the most shallow, fake women I've ever met for the entire time we've known each other," she said. "You and Zane, I don't know where you find them. All they care about is their next plastic surgery appointment and being on a red carpet with whoever will take them. There's no quality there."

"No, but it's easy," he said. "They don't expect anything from me."

"You're selling yourself so short," she said. "You're one of the best people I know. I don't know why you try and hide that, and keep yourself so locked up. The image that you put out to the world—this aloof, angry guy—is not who you are at all. I don't get it."

"That's not what I do," he said, shocked at her words. "Or at least not what I mean to do. Sometimes I just get uncomfortable and don't know how to act."

"Whether you mean it or not, it's what you do," she said. "You always look like you have a chip on your shoulder. You give one-word answers and always stick with Zane, so you don't have to talk to reporters. You ignore anyone you don't know, and half the people you do."

"Wow. I had no idea I was so horrible."

"You're not," she said. "It's almost like you're wildly insecure. Which is so weird, because you're one of the most gorgeous men I've ever seen. And you're also secretly really nice."

"Thanks," he said. "Want to get married and have babies?"

She threw a pillow at him. "Knock it off. I'm being serious; you should give Holly a chance. Go out with a real person for once, let her see who you are."

"And if she doesn't like me?"

"Then move on," she said. "You're both here for the holiday, just have fun. Let yourself be open to the possibility. It could be nothing, but I saw a spark there that I think is worth investigating."

"You going to give Mike a chance?"

"No," she said, shaking her head. "That's not at all what he wants, and I'm nowhere near ready for a relationship."

"You give good advice," he said. "Might be a good idea to take some of it yourself."

"I'll consider it if you ask her out," she said. "We made a deal, and I did my share, but you haven't done your part yet."

He finished his wine, setting the empty glass down on the table next to him. "You're right, I do need to follow through," he said. "Now, let's see if we can get some sleep."

"Here?" Natalie looked surprised, staring at him.

He shrugged. "Why not? We slept down here the night I arrived, remember? These couches are comfortable; we have a fire going and blankets. And maybe being here together will help."

"Thank you for not saying sleeping together," she said with a quiet laugh.

"You said it, not me," he teased her. "I always knew you wanted to."

"Go to sleep." She laughed softly. "And thank you."

"Anytime," he said, yawning and letting his eyes close. Maybe Natalie was right, and the only way to get some peace was to try with Holly. Because he knew, deep down, that what kept him awake tonight was the look in her eyes as she watched his lips approach hers. And the deep regret he felt for not taking advantage of the opportunity to kiss her.

Chapter 9

"Morning," Holly said as she entered the busy kitchen. Charlie was gobbling down a bowl of cereal at the island, Izzie settled against his chest. Jake and Shea were kissing by the coffee maker—a display she didn't need after a night spent thinking about a kiss that didn't happen. "If you two lovebirds don't mind, I am in desperate need of some caffeine."

"Sorry." Shea laughed. "You're being grumpy."

"I didn't sleep well," she admitted.

"Try having an infant sleeping next to you," Shea said. "And I'm not even talking about Jake."

"Hey!" Jake objected as Charlie laughed.

"I'm only teasing," she said. "It's gotten much better with Rex."

"He's helping you sleep?" Holly asked Jake, curious about the impact the service dog was having.

"Yes," he said with a nod. "He wakes me up if a nightmare starts, so I can't get too far into it that it's a struggle to come back."

"I'm glad it's working out," she said, smiling at her brother-in-law.

"Me too. I was worried the weeks away at training would be for nothing. Especially since it was during Shea's pregnancy. And when Charlie and I were getting back into a good place."

"Worked out for me," Charlie said. "I always wanted a dog."

"Maybe we can get another one for you," Shea suggested. "We already live in chaos with a teenager and an infant, might as well throw a puppy into the mix."

"Don't say that too loud; Patrick will be here in ten minutes with a rescue," Charlie laughed. "Who wants the baby? I have to get to school."

"I'll drop you," Jake said. "I'll see you ladies later." He kissed his wife and daughter and clipped on Rex's leash before following his son out the door, leaving the sisters alone in a quiet kitchen.

"It's weird when they leave every morning," Shea said. "It goes from all this life and noise to quiet. Unless this one is in a mood."

"She's an angel," Holly said. "I'm so glad I get to be here for her first Christmas. Thank you for letting me stay with you."

"Are you kidding? You're welcome here anytime. I'm so happy you're here," Shea said, her eyes welling up.

"Don't cry! I wasn't trying to trigger your hormones," she said, feeling badly about upsetting her sister.

"Everything triggers my hormones," Shea sighed. "I do wish Mom and Dad were staying here too, but they keep saying they don't want to crowd us. They've been so busy since they arrived, I feel like we've barely seen them. Ben and Stella are going to dinner with them later, and they went to Christmas Bingo at the senior center the other night."

"What's Christmas Bingo?"

"I have no idea," Shea said with a shrug. "But speaking of Christmas, thanks for pitching in so much for the youth center and the fundraising. Not to mention the jackets and supplies you said Natalie bought. This is going to be the best holiday ever in Windsor Peak. I can't wait for the Holiday Ball."

"The what?" Holly cut herself a piece of the coffee cake that Stella had baked and sent home with them the day before. Jake had told her that they should expect treats almost daily before the holidays, as his stepmother loved baking on a normal day, never mind the Christmas season. Jake and Shea had laughed, saying that Stella never seemed to step out of the kitchen between Thanksgiving and New Years, yet didn't want her and Ben to eat the treats.

"Did I not mention it to you? On the Saturday night of the Holiday Festival there is a ball," Shea said. "They hold it at the inn every year. It's so popular that they've almost outgrown the room there. I think they had to turn people away."

"What does it raise money for?"

"Primarily the youth center," Shea said. "But also, the animal shelter and some other small charities. I was hoping to get the organization that we got Rex from involved, but Patrick decided he would do something separate for them. That way the money raised at the ball will stay here in Windsor Peak."

"That's incredible," Holly said, her mind spinning. The event space at Liam's new property would easily hold several hundred people, and they had everything there that would be needed. "Do you think if we could offer a bigger space, you could get more people? Would that upset the organizers?"

"The inn is packed all weekend and short staffed, from what I hear," Shea said. "I'm sure they would be able to use the room for something else that would be easier to deal with. But there is no other space available."

"Let me see what I can do," Holly promised. "Do you mind if I borrow your car again?"

Shea tossed her the keys and Holly was on her way to grab her jacket when her phone chimed with an incoming text message from an unknown number.

Are you free? Can we meet for a coffee?

Three small dots appeared and then a second message. It's Liam.

Her stomach fluttered, and she wrote and deleted responses as she walked to the car. Finally, she settled on one and hit send before she could change her mind.

Yes, I was just about to come talk to you. Want me to pick you up?

Three dots appeared again before he sent his agreement, so she started the car and drove the short distance to Patrick's. Liam was standing outside on the porch when she pulled in, blowing into his bare hands.

"You should get some gloves," she said when he got in. "We should have thought of that last night."

"Last night was shopping for the kids," he said. "I'll grab some today."

"Did you need to talk to me about something?"

"What do you mean?" He looked at her quizzically.

"When you asked about getting coffee," she said. "I assumed that wasn't just a need for caffeine."

"Oh, no," he said. "We have that list from last night, and I feel like everyone else is so busy. I thought maybe we could look at it and see what we could check off."

"They were all so happy that you found a space," she said, pulling into a parking spot on Main Street. "I wish you had told them that you bought it, you deserve praise for that."

"I don't need praise," he said, walking to meet her on the sidewalk. "I get enough of that in my real life. And besides, they'll all find out when the new building opens and I'm still kicking around."

"You think you'll stay here?"

"I don't know," he said. "It's nice to be able to just walk around somewhat normally. But I think I underestimated the cold. Somehow, when I'm skiing or sitting in a lodge, the snow seems fun. This cold is just another level."

"I agree," she said, shivering. "But it's perfect for the holidays."

They ordered their coffees and claimed a small table in the back corner, where Liam could sit and not be seen. While she gathered some napkins, he had pulled out the notes from the night before.

"Before we start on that," she said, nodding at the paper. "Shea mentioned this morning that the annual Holiday Ball is the Saturday of the festival weekend. Apparently, it's a big fundraiser for the youth center, and some other local charities. It's gotten so big that they had to turn people away this year, but

I was thinking that maybe we could move it to your place? The event space would be perfect, and then people can see where their money is going. Plus, having more people means raising more money, which is needed after the fire."

"That sounds good." He nodded in agreement. "What do we need to do to make that happen?"

"Talk to the inn manager," she said. "I don't want to step on their toes. I thought we could check to see if they could cater it, assuming they've already ordered the supplies?"

"Or we could ask if Kendra and Zoe could do it, and just buy the food off the Inn," he suggested. "Let's talk to everyone when we leave here."

"Okay, so where are we on this?" she said, gesturing to the list they had made for the youth center.

"When we got back last night, Patrick, Natalie and I divided up what's needed and got to work on those," he said. "Nat is taking care of all the outside activities and wanted to get things for a dance studio and for baking. Her choices, I wasn't being sexist, I swear. Nat just thought there was enough space to do some cooking or baking lessons in the house, since the kitchen is so big. She already asked Zoe about volunteering some time there, and she'll talk her into it. Patrick is getting all the sports equipment, and I said I would get games, study materials, and some computer stations. Plus, video games, and some of those virtual reality systems. The kids will love them."

"They also could break easily," she warned him. "Don't give them more than the town can afford to replace."

"You're right," he said. "I'm thinking instant gratification, but maybe gaming systems are better that they can share, rather than something that's done alone."

"What about setting up a small lending library? Where kids can grab a book to read if they want, even trade a book for one on the shelf so it's always full."

"That's a great idea." He smiled at her, and she felt it warm her from the inside out even more than her hot drink had.

"I'm a bookworm, so that would have appealed to me," she shared.

"Me too," he said.

"You were? That's not at all how I pictured you as a kid."

"I was definitely not like this as a kid; or even a teenager," he said, gesturing at his body. "This came way too late for me to be considered cool."

She considered him, then shook her head. "I'm sorry, but I don't buy it. That seems like a good story to tell Jimmy Kimmel, but I bet you came out of the womb perfect."

He laughed, and she felt a sense of satisfaction for making his dimples appear naturally. "Not even close," he said. "I'll find some pictures to show you. Not only was I the smallest kid in class, but I also wore glasses, had braces for about three years, and was smart enough to have to skip a grade."

"When did you become—" she waved her hand at him— "*this.*"

"Hopefully, by *that,* you are complimenting me, which I live for," he said with a grin. "I grew rapidly after I turned fifteen.

Got the braces off at sixteen, after I had discovered the gym. By the time I went back to school for my senior year, everyone thought I was a new kid."

"Seriously?"

"Yes. I had no friends, really. And trust me when I say that not one single girl looked at me, up until that moment," he shared. "That year I got the starring role in the school play, and I had the acting bug from that moment on."

"No college?"

"Much to my parents' dismay, no. I had some scholarship opportunities, but they were for academics, not to be a theater major. I decided to head straight to Hollywood and see what would happen."

"It worked out well for you, at least."

"Not at first," he said. "The first few years were brutal. I worked as a valet, waited tables, bartended, did whatever I could to make a little money. And I went to audition after audition; until one day I got lucky. A casting director sat at my bar, and we got to talking. She was from the same area I had grown up in, and she liked me enough to ask me to come in for a read. I expected to get some small part, maybe be killed off immediately. Instead, I found my face on a movie poster a year later, and my whole life changed."

"That explains why you want to give back," Holly said. "Make sure these kids can enjoy their youth; and have a safe space for whatever makes them happy."

"Exactly," he said. "Plus, it makes me feel like less of a selfish grinch."

She grinned at him. "I don't think I called you that exactly, but we still have a lot of work to do. Just wearing a Santa hat one time doesn't infuse you with the Christmas spirit."

"What's next on that list?"

"Hmm." She tapped her lip as she considered. "Let's do the decorations today, get the place looking festive. We'll have to start with Christmas trees and wreaths, which we can do easily. The lights and ornaments we might need to track down."

"Alright," he said, pushing back his chair. "Let's get Project Christmas started."

"That sounds too clinical," she said. "We need a new name for it."

He laughed, gesturing for her to walk in front of him. "I'll add it to the list."

Chapter 10

"What about this one?" Holly asked, pointing to a tall tree. They had been circling the tree lot for a half hour while he debated all the tree options, and she had stayed patient. Her cheeks were pink and her eyes bright, and it was all he could do to not request a re-do on their mistletoe kiss. He forced himself to look at the tree she was pointing at, which was the best one they had seen.

"Yes, that's perfect," he said. "Should we get a few more?"

"We have seen every tree out here," she said, glancing around the large lot. "Where else do you want to put them?"

"This one in the event space," he suggested. "It's huge and will look great. And let's get one for the main house and one for the apartment, just in case I decide to stay there."

"Do you think you will?"

"Not sure," he said. "I just want to keep it as an option. Right now, it's good to stay close to Nat."

She felt a twinge of jealousy at the mention of the gorgeous movie star, but pushed it aside. Where had that even come from? She and Liam were barely even friends. Yes, he was nice to look at and much nicer than he had appeared at their first, and second, meetings, but he wasn't interested in her. She forced herself to focus on the tree he was examining. "That looks like an option," she said.

"Okay, let's get those two, and I'll just ask the person who works here to grab a second one like this," he said.

"Do they work for you?" She raised an eyebrow at him.

"No, but they probably have a better sense of the options than I do."

"Still," she insisted. "It's easier on them if we just go up and request the ones you want. Then we have to figure out how to get them there."

"They don't deliver?" He looked shocked, and she had to laugh.

"We're in a small town in Vermont, not Los Angeles or New York City," she said. "But we can ask about options."

They approached the small checkout counter, which held a vat of complimentary hot chocolate. She poured them each a cup while he charmed the older woman working there, arranging for her son to bring the trees up to the house when he finished for the night. She sold him three tree stands and skirts, tree toppers, and wreaths for each window, and then gave him strict instructions for watering the trees before taking his money.

"That felt like taking an exam in school," he said under his breath as they walked away. "I hope I passed."

"We'll find out if she trusts you with her trees if the son shows up later," she guessed. "In the meantime, we should go find lights and ornaments."

"I feel like we could pay a professional to do that part."

She stopped walking, and he got a few steps away before realizing she was no longer next to him. When he turned to look at what she was doing, she pointed at him. "You will not Grinch this. We are decorating those trees; it's part of Project Christmas."

"I still hate the name," he said. "And I feel like it's going to take forever. How do you even get all the lights on there to look perfect?"

"It's not supposed to look perfect," she said, starting to walk again. "It's supposed to look like a family almost got brought to tears over the stringing of them before they started liking each other again with the ornaments. When the boxes come out and all the memories surface, that heals the trauma from getting the lights figured out."

"I think I'm in way over my head."

"Most likely, but we're going to do our best," she said. "Now, it's time we find the lights and ornaments, and see where we're at with everything else."

As she drove to a box store in the next town over, he checked his phone. "My assistant arranged for all the equipment that to be delivered tomorrow," he told her. "He also thought to order moveable walls, whatever that means. But he says we'll be able to divide up the larger spaces and make it more cozy, and then take them out before the ball on Saturday."

"The ball! I almost forgot; we need to stop at the inn and talk to them."

"Let's do it on our way back into town," he suggested. "The earlier we hit a big store the better. It's less likely I'll get swarmed."

"I didn't think of that," she admitted. "You can stay in the car if you want?"

"And miss this step of Holiday Hoopla? No, thank you."

"Hoopla isn't the right word." She laughed. "Mission Christmas?"

"That definitely doesn't work, but we'll keep trying."

She flipped on a radio station that was playing Christmas music and hummed along with the songs as they rode in comfortable silence. As they approached the neighboring town, Liam gestured to a sandwich shop and suggested they grab lunch to eat in the car. It looked quiet inside, with just one person at the counter waiting for an order.

"Want me to go in and grab lunch?" Holly offered at his reluctance to go inside.

"No, it doesn't look like there are many people in there at all," he said. "Let's grab it to go, okay?"

She agreed; and soon they were back on the road, eating their sandwiches in comfortable silence. He was done in record time, then downed a bottle of water before packing all his trash up into the bag they had been given. She was oddly touched by his care to not leave trash behind in Shea's car, but kept her thoughts to herself.

"Are you sure you are up for this?" she asked as she pulled into the parking lot of the store.

"It's good for the ego," he told her. "And I have a hat, plus the hood of my sweatshirt. It's like I'm invisible."

"Or a shoplifter," she said.

He laughed as he climbed out of the car, and then stopped to look at her. "You make me laugh."

"I'm not sure if that's a good thing or a bad thing," she retorted.

He grabbed a cart out of the return bin and started walking towards the store entrance. "I can't figure that out either," he said over his shoulder. "I guess we'll see."

They entered the store and managed to get to the Christmas section before anyone seemed to notice him. One young mother, with two kids in her cart, did a double take as she grabbed a box of lights off the shelf in front of him. "Are you—" she stuttered, staring at him.

"No, he gets that a lot," Holly tried, before Liam smiled and stepped forward.

"Hey, nice to meet you," he said. "Merry Christmas."

"Can we take a picture? My friends are never going to believe this. They see Patrick Burrows all the time, and I never do. This will make us even," she gushed. Liam smiled and took a picture with her, then with her kids, before she wandered off, looking starstruck.

"Did that help get you back into balance?" Holly teased him as the woman walked away.

"Not quite, but it helps," he said, preening into the reflection of a large silver star decoration.

Before Holly knew what happened, women appeared from every possible angle and filled the aisle, all trying to get to Liam. She felt herself being pushed back away from him, and watched as he was getting grabbed and groped by hands in every direction.

A staff member approached, and Holly grabbed his attention. "Do you have security here? Can we get some help?"

The man surveyed the situation, his eyes bugging when he saw Liam in the center of it. "Right away, ma'am," he said, disappearing down a different aisle.

Within a few minutes, two burly men appeared, moving through the women with authority until they reached Liam. They cleared the space around him and then gestured to the cart, which was still relatively empty.

"We just came to grab some lights and ornaments," Liam explained, pointing at her. "If you ladies wouldn't mind giving us a chance to do that I would really appreciate it."

The security guards waved the women away, and soon, they were alone in the aisle, with a guard on either side. "That was intense," she whispered to him. "I can't imagine what that feels like for you."

He shrugged, looking far away in thought, and she saw lipstick marks on his cheek and on his hoodie. His hand was bleeding slightly, where it looked like someone had grabbed him with a fingernail. She winced as she reached for it, examining it before pulling a Band-Aid out of her purse and putting it on.

"Are you going to kiss it too?"

She paused, looking up at him, seeing the half smile on his face and the light back in his eyes. Slowly, she raised his hand to her lips and pressed them to the Band-Aid, making him smile all the way. "I have other—"

"I'll stop you right there." She laughed. "Let's get what we need and get out of here before a riot breaks out. That was not fun."

"I'm sorry," he said quietly. "I didn't think it would be that bad, and I really didn't think what that would be like for you."

"No need to apologize," she said. "I'm fine. But I do want to get out of this store."

They filled the cart quickly, then followed the guard to a register that had been roped off for him. The crowd of people watching them made her skin crawl, but Liam acted as though he was happy, chatting with the attendant. She realized that the man in front of her right now was not the same one who had been with her in the field of trees, when they were alone. It was as if he had donned a mask, or gone into character, and put the real Liam out of sight. The thought of that happening to him constantly, and the need to be on guard all the time, had her resolving to make this the best holiday of his life. He was looking out for the kids of Windsor Peak to make sure they had a safe and happy place, and she would do the same thing for him.

Chapter 11

His heart rate had settled down to normal by the time the car approached the inn, but he still felt some trepidation about going into public again. The scene in the store had been unexpected, and seeing the startled look in Holly's eyes had made it even worse. He had let his guard down, lost in the moment with her, and he needed to do better. Maybe now she would understand the need to hand things off to an assistant, or to have items delivered. He felt a foul mood approaching and tried to push it aside, but the dark cloud refused to diffuse, and he slammed the car door when they were parked.

"What's wrong?" Holly asked, jumping at the noise as she climbed out of the car.

"Nothing."

"Nothing? Don't pout. You're clearly pissed at something, and since I'm the only one here, I'm guessing it's me."

"I told you I shouldn't go into stores," he fumed.

"Actually, you didn't," she said. "You said you wanted to have someone else order it, and then you told me it would be fine because you had your disguise. Don't blame me for what happened."

"Hard to look anywhere else." He couldn't stop the words from coming out, even though he regretted it instantly. He had to get the anger out.

She stared at him for a long minute, then closed her own door quietly and threw the keys to him. "You can either stay out here in the car while I talk to the manager, or you can take the car back and I'll get a ride. Your choice, I don't care either way. If you're gone when I come out, I'll leave you alone for the duration of your stay."

He watched as she walked away and resisted the urge to follow her. He really didn't want to be in public again today, especially in a building filled with tourists, so he stayed put. As she climbed the stairs and disappeared into the front door, he felt the fight go out of him. She really hadn't had any idea of what would happen, and he should have been more vocal in it. He was just so used to people taking care of things for him and being in his world that he had assumed she understood. Unlocking the car, he sank back into the passenger seat and tried to reset his mood.

As he sat and waited, he watched everyone as they walked through the town square or on the sidewalks toward the shops. Everyone looked happy and festive, calling out greetings to each other as they passed. This was a town where friends and strangers were welcomed with open arms, and everyone seemed to have an ease about them. Couples were holding hands, friends greeted each other with hugs, and babies were being pushed in strollers. It was so normal and happy that he had to wonder what his life would have been if he hadn't followed the path he was on. Would he be in a similar town, pushing a carriage while his wife talked to friends?

When Holly came back outside, she saw the car and seemed to steel her shoulders before walking his way. She climbed back into the driver's seat without meeting his eyes, and it made him feel even worse.

"I'm really sorry," he said quietly. "Please, look at me for a second."

She turned her big green eyes onto him, and something inside of him shifted. He cared about her, and truly felt badly that he had hurt her feelings and misdirected his anger at her. "Please, forgive me. I was wrong, and I feel terrible."

She shrugged, and he felt a wave of disappointment. "It's fine," she said. "Do you have the keys?"

"Where are we going now?" he asked, hoping she had another festive chore for them.

"I thought I would drop you off at your house, and I'll go check on Shea," she responded. "You need to wait for the trees, and I have some stuff to do."

"You're mad, and you're perfectly entitled to be so," he said. "But please, don't give up on me."

She pulled out of the parking space, avoiding his eyes again. "I'm just going to be busy," she said. "And I'm sure you have other people who can take care of all this. I was wrong to try and force you to do something you didn't want to do."

"But I do! That's what I'm trying to say," he said. "I'm not good when someone isn't writing a script for me."

He saw the hint of a smile on her face before she sobered again. "Still, we aren't friends. We're both just here for a short time, and I think maybe it would be better to give up on this plan."

"Just help me decorate the trees," he begged. "I don't know what I'm doing, and I need you. Please."

She sighed, then glanced at him before returning her eyes to the road. "Fine."

When they got to his new house, he insisted she stay inside where it was warm while he carried in the purchases. It was the least he could do, after how he had acted. She stood, looking uncertain, as he brought in bag after bag. When he went out for the last one, he made a quick decision, pulling out his cell phone and firing off a text before putting it back into his pocket.

"We should do the outdoor lights and wreaths while the sun is still out," she said. "Do you know if you have a ladder?"

"I think I saw one out in the barn," he said. "I'll run down and check. I want to suggest hiring someone to do the dangerous stuff, but I'm afraid you'll think I'm ridiculous."

She shot him a look. "I would."

He jogged to the barn, dragging back a heavy ladder that he propped up outside the front door. As he looked at how high the roof line was, he opted to keep to himself that climbing that high was the last thing he wanted to do. But if he insisted on hiring someone to do it she would leave, and he couldn't have that.

Holly came out holding boxes of lights and frowned at him. "We need to start at the end of the house."

"Oh. Okay, let me move it." He dragged the ladder down, propping it up. Holly joined him, handing him a strip of stick-on light clips. "So, these just—" he trailed off, looking at the clips and feeling like a total idiot.

"Just stick them along the trim there," she said, pointing above his head. "Then I'll hand you the lights to string through.

When we get near the windows, we'll do the wreath while you're up there. I'll walk you through it."

They worked for over an hour, dragging the ladder down the house as they got the lights and wreaths in place. Just when they finished, a new car pulled in the driveway and Holly looked over. "Were you expecting someone?"

"I ordered us some food," he told her. "I was hoping you would have dinner with me. And I got hot chocolate, which I think we both need right now."

"Liam—"

"Please," he said quietly. "Forgive me. I know I was a jerk. I know I'm spoiled and self-involved, and I don't deserve your time or attention. But I like being with you, and I hope you will give me another chance to do better."

The delivery driver was unloading items as Liam rushed to open the door, unable or unwilling to wait to hear Holly's answer. The fact that she wasn't walking toward her car was a good sign, and when she followed him inside and removed her coat and boots, he felt hopeful. After he sent the driver off with a healthy tip for the rush order, he turned back to her.

She smiled shyly at him, and he felt his heart lift. "Okay, I'll stay. You went to all this trouble, and I made you risk your life on the ladder. Seems the least I can do is eat some of this food."

He grinned at her, realizing he hadn't been this excited and nervous about spending time with a woman since his first date. It had been his senior year of high school, and the most popular girl in school had agreed to go to the movies with him. He had been unsure of himself the entire time, worried he would do the wrong thing. At the end of the night, when they had kissed goodnight, he had felt like he had won the jackpot.

And that was nothing compared to how he felt just having Holly agree to stay for dinner.

Chapter 12

Enjoying a meal by a lit-up Christmas tree with a movie star was not something Holly had ever envisioned herself doing, and yet here she was. The truck containing all the trees had arrived just after they unpacked the food and wine Liam had ordered, and they accepted the help of the two teenage delivery boys to get the trees into the stands. The trees were enormous, and she found herself grateful that the two young men were able to help guide them into the stand, when one would then disappear underneath to secure it. The largest tree had required all three men to carry it, and she was glad that she wasn't the one trying to make sure it would stay put. She didn't see how much Liam had tipped each of them, but both boys had gone a little bug-eyed at the cash and thanked him profusely. He had also patiently posed for selfies with them and sent video messages to each of their girlfriends, which they claimed would win them major bonus points.

Once the boys had left and they were faced with bare trees sitting in stands, they had agreed to get the first tree strung with lights before eating. The process had induced much needed laughter—subtle at first, but then more explosive—as Liam continued to get tangled in the wires. It had also included their hands brushing each time they passed the lights around the tree, and she was trying hard to ignore the spark every time it happened. The earlier tension had softened or, perhaps, turned into an awareness of a possible attraction between them. Whatever it was, she felt her wariness fading away and started to enjoy his company again.

Liam had suggested they eat picnic-style by the tree, so she had found a blanket to spread on the hardwood floor while he worked on getting a fire started in the fireplace. They warmed up the food together and opened a bottle of wine before settling on the floor together.

Holly took in the number of containers that surrounded them as Liam piled food on both of their plates. "You ordered enough food for ten people." She laughed as he kept adding things to her plate.

"I wasn't sure what you'd like," he said. "And I was worried you'd leave, and I'd be alone, eating my emotions away along with my tears."

"Oh, please," she said, rolling her eyes. "Like Liam Dorsey would cry over me."

"Why wouldn't I?" He looked so genuinely confused that she could only laugh again.

"Because you're you," she said, waving a hand at him. "And I'm just me."

"I happen to like you," he argued.

"Okay," she said, rolling her eyes. "Moving on. Tomorrow, we should be in good shape to have the kids here after school. Jake said he can get his guys to install those moveable walls, assuming they get delivered on time."

"My assistant said they would be here early," he said. "I asked Jake to put a crew up here as a priority; they should be arriving before seven."

"And a ton of volunteers will come by to help with everything else," she went on. "The kids will walk over after school. Shea said the school is so relieved to have somewhere for them to go. If they had to keep them at the school after hours for months, it would take a toll on the staff and the building. Not to mention, the kids want to be in a different setting than they were all day."

"I'm sure they have energy to burn," he said. "Especially with the holidays coming up. Speaking of, and in the spirit of my festive training, why is it that you love Christmas so much?"

"It's just magical," she said. "People are kinder to each other around the holidays, more willing to give to those less fortunate. Everyone smiles more, and the world just seems a happier place. Plus, it's my birthday."

"It is?" He looked surprised.

"My name is Holly." She laughed. "I can't believe you didn't put that together. My birthday is Christmas Eve."

"That must have been tough as a kid," he said. "Did you mind?"

"Not too much," she admitted. "I don't like to be the center of attention, so it worked for me. Everyone was opening presents at the same time, not just me with everyone watching. I think it was better for me that way."

"I can see that," he said.

"What about you? When is your birthday?"

"July," he said. "Not only was I an ugly duckling in school, but I was also one of the youngest. It wasn't easy."

"I'm sorry," she said. "It's hard to picture you like that now."

"I'll have to find a picture for you," he said. "Every once in a while, the magazines publish them. Like a 'can you believe this' type of feature."

"That's mean."

"I like to think of it as giving the next generation hope," he said. "Since you're double-dipping with Christmas and your birthday, what's the best gift you've gotten?"

"It's really not about that," she said. "I'm more of a giver. I don't receive gifts well. But I love to give someone a gift I know they'll love."

"How about a favorite memory?"

"One Christmas, we got snowed in," she shared. "We were supposed to go to my aunt's house, and we wanted to stay home instead to play with our new toys. When it snowed on Christmas Eve, it was like Santa had delivered an extra gift. The electricity was out, so we spent the day by the fire, eating whatever we didn't need to cook. My parents even let us roast marshmallows on the fire to make s'mores. My mother made us all turkey sandwiches for dinner, and she was sad because she felt like we should have a big meal, but we loved it. She cheered up once we were all sitting in front of the fire, just us, and no one was complaining one bit."

"Kind of like us right now," he said with a smile.

She held up a piece of sushi, which he had managed to order despite there being no restaurant that served it in Windsor Peak. "This is far from a turkey sandwich."

"Still, the picnic and fire part," he said.

"True," she said softly. She pushed the food away, realizing how stuffed she was, and sipped at her wine before looking back at him. "Want to try my favorite thing to do?"

"Sure," he said.

"Lie down like this," she said, flipping onto her back so her head was under the Christmas tree. The lights above her twinkled through the branches, and the smell of balsam tickled her nose.

Liam settled in next to her, sliding so close that their shoulders were touching. "This is nice," he said. "It's like being in a hidden forest."

"Exactly." She smiled, happy that he appreciated it the way she did. They enjoyed the silence for a moment, and then she felt his hand embrace hers between their two bodies.

"Holly?"

"Yes?" She felt breathless suddenly, feeling the heat of his hand under hers.

"You seem to think you're not enough for me," he said quietly. "And I think the opposite might be true."

"What do you mean?"

"I don't think I'm a good enough man for you," he explained. "But I'd really like to be someone worthy of you."

"Liam…" She turned to look at him and was mesmerized by his eyes. They were focused on hers and then dropped to her lips, reminding her of the near-kiss the night before. "Don't doubt yourself. Look at everything you've accomplished."

"Oh, that's nothing. Honestly, I can't believe I get paid as much as I do for something so fun," he said. "What I mean is that I don't seek out opportunities to do good, like Patrick does. I've been pretty selfish for a lot of years, and I hope to change that. Someone like you, who does things to help people every day... You need a man like that."

"First of all, I appreciate the compliment, but I also love what I do. It's fun to meet new people and to do what I love. I think that's the goal for most people, to be happy at work," she said. "Secondly—"

"Yes?" He watched her, patiently waiting for her to continue.

She debated her words, and then finally decided to just go for it. When else would she be in this situation with him? She couldn't possibly be imagining the heat between them, and he clearly needed a nudge. "Do you think there is mistletoe in this tree?"

He laughed, and she felt it shake her slightly. "I honestly don't care," he said, pulling her closer. "But I like how your mind works."

His lips finally settling on hers became her new favorite Christmas memory.

Chapter 13

The morning passed in a blur, with a flurry of activity in all of the buildings as Jake's crew and a team of volunteers prepared for the students to arrive. A food delivery truck had backed up the driveway, dropping off supplies for the kitchen staff that had relocated from the youth center. They had been thrilled to find the extravagant kitchen where they could make meals to send home with the kids, as well as the second one in the house for backup. According to the manager, they were used to piecing together old and broken equipment.

Jake and his workers had quickly installed the portable walls, separating the space into smaller rooms. Some kept the tables to be used as study space or to do art projects on, while others were designated for other purposes. Jake suggested a music room and had offered to install some panels to contain sound, so they were currently working on that, while Liam sourced instruments from the small shop in town. Truck after truck arrived, carrying sports equipment, craft materials, easels and paint, books, and the outdoor clothing and toys they had shopped for.

When school let out and students began streaming in, Liam stood with all the volunteers and watched them run around the property in excitement. Some of the younger kids needed encouragement to explore, and a few chose to settle in quietly with their backpacks rather than join in. Liam took note of them, wanting to make sure that all of the kids felt welcome and secure here. He especially paid attention to the kids who had lined up outside the dining area, waiting to put the bagged meal into their backpack before grabbing a snack and moving on to activities. Seeing kids be hungry was going to be a challenge, and he was determined that it didn't happen on his watch.

"Mr. Liam?"

He glanced down to find a young boy, who couldn't be more than six, standing in front of him. He hunched down to be eye level with him and smiled. "Hey."

"Thank you for doing this," the boy said with a lisp.

"What's your name?"

"Robbie," the little boy said. "They said you're in movies."

"I am." Liam smiled. "What do you do?"

"I just go to school," he said.

"School is very important."

"Yeah." Robbie kicked at a mound of snow and looked around before leaning closer. "Do you believe in Santa Claus? Because some of the big kids on the bus said he's not real, but if you believe, then I know they's lying."

"I do. Do you believe in magic, Robbie?" He waited until the boy nodded before continuing. "Not everyone does. Some people say that a magic trick is just a trick; they don't want to believe that something happened they don't understand. That's what Santa is: magic."

"Do you think he'll bring me something?" The little boy looked hopeful but also on the verge of tears, and Liam realized he might be in over his head.

"I promise he will," he said, silently vowing to make sure it happened.

Robbie beamed at him, making him feel better than any award show or movie premiere had ever made him feel. "Thanks, Mr. Liam. I'm going to go get something to eat before it's all gone."

As he ran off, Liam caught the eye of one of the youth center workers and waved her over. She was young, probably a high school student who had her first job, and approached him shyly.

He smiled at her, holding out a hand to shake as she got closer. "Hi, I'm Liam."

"Oh, we all know who you are," she gushed before blushing. "I mean, hi, I'm Grace."

"Grace, it's nice to meet you," he said. "Do you know Robbie over there?"

She looked where he pointed before nodding. "Yes, Robbie Henry. They moved to town over the summer, I think."

"Could you do me a favor? I noticed his jacket is too small to be zipped, and he didn't have a hat or gloves," he said. "We got a whole delivery of supplies, so I'd like to make sure he goes home with winter clothes that will fit him."

"Of course," she said.

"Thanks," he said.

She turned and crossed to where Robbie was tucking his packed meal into his bag, and took his hand to lead him to where the gear was stored. Once they disappeared, Liam left the building and went to look in on the barn, where a rowdy game of dodgeball was taking place. Outside, kids decked in new snowpants raced around with sleds and threw snowballs at each other, and laughter seemed to warm the air around him. He participated in a snowball fight and helped to make a snowman before begging off, telling the kids he needed to warm up.

He toed off his boots and peeled off the wet outerwear he wore before venturing further into the main house. The main living room had been transformed into a large office for the few full-time employees, and he had encouraged them to use the kitchen and any other space they needed. One main floor bedroom had been converted into a nurse's office, and another into a small area with books and desks for kids who needed a break from the fun.

The director of the youth center was in the kitchen, making a cup of tea when he came in, and she smiled at him. "The kids are going to talk about that for years," she said. "Beating a superhero in a snowball fight is not something they will forget."

"I'll have to get Patrick up here as well." He laughed. "Maybe even Nat. Then, they can beat two or three of us. Maybe us against them."

"Oh, they would love that," she said. "Thank you again for helping organize all of this. I can't believe how quickly it all came together."

"I was talking to a little boy, Robbie Henry," he said. "I asked Grace to help him find new winter gear; the stuff he was wearing was too small. And he only had sneakers on, not boots. Is that normal?"

"The Henrys have had a tough year," she confided in him. "His dad lost his job in Burlington, and his mom had been sick.

I think the treatments drained their savings, from what I've heard. Robbie is here on financial aid, so I know things are tough for them. I know his dad has been applying for every job he can think of, but there's not a lot around here. They moved down to save on rent and have been staying with her parents. The house is very small, and I don't know how they are managing, but they are somehow. I'm sorry, it's not like me to be going on like this. I've just been so concerned about them. They are very nice people; I see them at church and am always trying to find ways to help. I send Robbie home with extra food every day because I don't think they would accept it if I were to offer it to them."

"Do you know where they live?"

"I do," she said. She pulled a pen out of her pocket and wrote an address on a napkin before passing it to him.

"Thanks," he said, smiling at her as he stuffed it in his pocket. He looked around, seeing nothing for him to get involved with, before going back to put his wet boots and jacket back on.

The pickup truck that had come with the property had been serviced and returned to him, and he punched the address into his phone before climbing in. The truck was a far cry from his fleet of luxury vehicles in California, but it started right up and was safe to drive through the snowy roads.

He drove slowly down Main Street and then followed the map to the outskirts of town. He slowed even further as he neared the address he was given and crawled by the small house. It was tiny and clearly in need of repairs but looked well cared for. The driveway was shoveled, as was a path to the front door. A large woodpile was on the front porch, mostly covered with a tarp. The lights were on in one room, and he could see a neat kitchen through the window.

He turned around at the end of the street, heading back to Patrick's house. He needed help from his friends to figure out the best way to help Robbie's family, and then he had a certain nurse to convince to have a late dinner with him. Normally, he would be in need of some personal space after spending a full twelve hours with a woman. Holly was the opposite; he had missed her all day despite being with her until late the night before. He found himself checking his phone all day to respond quickly to her texts regaling him with tales of babysitting her niece. Although he wasn't sad to have missed the spit-up, he had oddly found himself missing the woman claiming to be covered in it. It was so out of character for him, to be thinking of a woman like this and wanting to get to know her, that he needed to see what could come of it.

Chapter 14

Infants were exhausting. Holly was tired in every part of her body and had showered twice while Izzy napped, since she had been covered in spit-up. How such a little baby could produce enough liquid to virtually cover her body was beyond comprehension, yet that's what it had felt like. Izzy slept for two-hour stretches between feedings and diaper changes, but the preparation and cleanup process filled that space, so Holly had only sat down when the baby was taking a bottle. She had no idea how Shea had managed for weeks, along with tending to the house, caring for Charlie, and maintaining a relationship with Jake.

Jake was the first home, arriving just after the Christmas lights had all turned on. He had promised Shea he would end his day early so that she could thoroughly enjoy her day of Christmas shopping and dinner with her friends. Shea had wanted Holly to join them, but she had insisted she wanted the time with her niece. Soon, she would be gone from Windsor Peak, and she wanted to relish the moments with the baby.

"Hey," Jake called over to her as he pulled his boots off. Rex sat patiently at his side, waiting until Jake moved into the room to follow. "How's my girl doing?"

"I'm doing great, but I think Shea might have a problem if I'm your girl," Holly quipped. Jake rolled his eyes at her and laughed. "Oh, Izzie! She's also doing great. How was your day?"

"Busy but fun," Jake said. "We did a lot of work at the property being used for the youth center. I don't know how

Liam convinced the owner to let the town use it, but it must have cost him a pretty penny. Not to mention all the things that arrived today; it was just truck after truck. And he insisted on paying me for my guys' time, even though I tried to volunteer us."

"He's turning out to be a good guy," Holly said. "I wasn't expecting that after our first meeting."

"The coffee thing?"

"Yeah, and just how he acted at Patrick's that first night. Kind of arrogant, you know?"

"I do," Jake said, nodding. "But Patrick comes off that way sometimes too, especially when he's uncomfortable. And you know he's the nicest guy on the planet, but the celebrity part gets to them sometimes. When it's just all of us hanging out, Patrick, Liam, and Natalie—and even Zane when he's here—they're just normal. They only get weird when they're unsure of new people or worried about their safety if a crowd were to form. I think it takes them all a while to get comfortable and let that guard down."

"That makes sense," she said. "Honestly, I was so mad about the coffee, that I didn't really give him a chance that night. But since then, he's been great."

"Do I sense a romance starting?" Jake teased, and she felt her cheeks turn red.

"Do you really want to talk about my love life?"

He held up two hands. "You're absolutely right. I've never had a sister, and I'm not sure how this all works, but it's a hard no. I don't want to know anything."

"Let's change the subject." She laughed. "How are things working out with Rex?"

The dog was lying at Jake's feet, and Holly knew that although he looked perfectly relaxed, if Jake's PTSD were to be triggered with a loud noise, the dog would instantly react. She had seen it happen once already, and Shea had shared that the dog had comforted Jake many times during the night.

Jake looked down at the dog before answering and almost appeared to be composing himself. "He's changed my life," he finally said. "For the better."

"That's amazing," Holly said, feeling herself get emotional.

Jake's struggles with PTSD were less visible to her, but she had spent many hours on the phone with Shea as she cried. Watching her husband battle the demons in his memories was excruciating for her sister, as well as everyone who cared about Jake. Knowing he had some relief, and seeing him smile more, was the best Christmas present anyone could have asked for.

"Here, let me take the baby," Jake said, standing to take her. "You must have better things to do than sit around with me. Charlie should be home from practice soon, and we can order pizza. You're welcome to join us if you'd like."

"Actually, Liam texted me a little while ago," she admitted. "I think I might head out with him if you think you'll be okay."

"Absolutely," Jake said. "I missed so much of Charlie's younger years; I'm soaking in every second with Izzy."

Holly made sure he was settled with the baby and then ran up the stairs, suddenly anxious to see Liam again. What Jake said about their first meeting made sense, and she had seen firsthand that her initial impression of Liam was completely wrong. Since that first day, he had been kind, giving, and fun to be around.

The attraction had been growing, and she had been so relieved the night before to realize that it wasn't one-sided. She was a little concerned that she was just an amusement to pass the time while he was in Vermont for the holidays, but she tried to push that thought away. Comparing herself to Natalie or any of the women she had seen on his arm in magazines wasn't going to end well, and she had to tell herself she was good enough. Maybe if she said it many times, it would start to sink in.

Jake was still settled on the couch with the sleeping baby when she jogged down the stairs. He glanced up as she came down, then cleared his throat. "Before you go, can I give you one piece of advice?"

"Sure."

"When Patrick became famous, it really thrust us all into the spotlight," he shared. "Pictures started showing up online, with people commenting constantly. He was already famous when Jenna died, and his manager pulled me aside one day to tell me not to look anymore. Don't read the comments, don't see what they're sharing. I enlisted and kind of forgot about it for years, but when I came home and started dating your sister, it all came back. Suddenly, pictures of all of us out at night were on social media, and I had to convince Shea not to pay attention to any of it."

"I remember that," Holly said. "She was really upset the first time, and I may have gotten into a few internet fights on her behalf."

"It would be a thousand times worse if you were seen as someone that Liam was dating," Jake said. "My advice is to stay off social media and certainly don't read any comments. It's going to be ugly, and you don't need that."

"Is there something out there now?" Holly had been so busy with Izzie all day; she hadn't scrolled through her usual feeds and had been ignoring all texts other than the ones from Liam and Shea.

Jake nodded and met her eyes with his level gaze. "There were some pictures taken when you were shopping."

"I wonder if Liam knows?"

"Probably not," Jake said. "Patrick never looks at that stuff, he has people who post for him and deal with the comments. I would guess they all handle it the same way. I would strongly suggest you do the same."

His words resonated in her head, along with her own fears about not being enough for Liam. She had to resist the urge to open Instagram instantly and see what people were saying about her, but she knew from Shea's experience that people would be nasty. Better to take Jake's advice and ignore it for now. She told herself to enjoy the moment let whatever was between them happen naturally, because it could turn out to be nothing more than friendship. And then she would have gotten herself worked up over nothing.

***

"I bought you a present," Liam said as she climbed into the truck. He had insisted on coming to pick her up and even walked to the door to get her. The chivalry and appearance of a date was not lost on her, and she glanced at the bag between them with excitement.

"That's so nice," she said. "But I feel bad that I don't have anything to give you."

"This is for both of us," he said. "Do you want to open it before or after dinner?"

"Hmm," she pondered. "I don't know. The anticipation is half the fun, right?"

He laughed as he clicked his seatbelt into place. "This might not be quite that big," he said. "Maybe you should open it, so it doesn't seem like a disappointment."

"Okay," she said. He watched as she pulled out the tissue paper, and she grinned at him when she saw what was inside. "Gingerbread houses?"

"A whole village," he said. "Plus, a train. Although the train is the same size as the houses, so that could present a problem to the residents. I thought we could do them after dinner, and then I had boxes' full delivered to the house so the kids can do their own tomorrow. Ours can be the inspiration."

"No pressure." She laughed. "It's almost like the holiday spirit has finally gotten a hold of you."

"A little bit," he said. "It's hard not to, with all the kids around talking about Santa and sharing their excitement. Plus, I realized today there are some kids in town whose parents might be struggling to provide, so I need to figure out how to help with that."

"You can't solve every problem," she said gently. "It's nice that you want to, but this town seems to look out for its own. As much fun as we're having, we're just visiting. We might need to leave some of the issues behind."

He frowned, glancing over at her before putting his eyes back on the road. "I don't think I can do that," he said. "I seem to have been fully engaged here."

"Are you thinking of staying after the holidays?"

"I'm not sure," he said, shrugging. "I really haven't thought about it much. I have a movie to film in a few months, assuming Natalie is doing okay. And some commercials I need to go overseas to shoot, but that's just a few weeks. Kicking around California feels boring in comparison to life here."

"Most people would say the opposite," she pointed out. "All the restaurants and parties, people to see and places to go."

"But Windsor Peak has karaoke each week," he countered. "How do you compete with that?"

"We do have Christmas karaoke coming up," she said. "I hope you're preparing."

"Practicing in the shower every day," he promised.

"Where are we going for dinner? I assumed we would be going to the Palace or getting takeout again," she asked as they got onto the highway.

"I wanted to actually take you out, since this is our first date."

"It is?"

"Yes," he said, almost sounding shy. "As long as that's okay with you."

"More than okay," she said, smiling at him. "Where are we going?"

"Patrick told me about this little place not far away. He said they go over the top decorating for Christmas, like an Elf threw up all over the place."

"I spent my day covered in spit-up, and now you want to use that as a reference before eating?"

"You're right. I take it back," he said. "Like elves had a wild party?"

"Better." She laughed. "I can't wait to see it."

Chapter 15

Liam led Holly into the small restaurant Patrick had recommended. He had become friendly with the owner, Wyatt, who had agreed to set up a table out of sight for Liam. The entire restaurant was decorated for the holidays, with ornaments hanging from the ceiling, menorahs on the windowsills, stockings hung on the chimney, and Christmas trees creating private nooks for the diners. Each table was strategically placed so the trees and giant poinsettias created a secluded area, and Wyatt led them to the most remote spot, in the corner near the fireplace.

"If anyone gives you a problem, just let me know," Wyatt said.

Liam nodded as he pulled out Holly's chair before shaking the other man's hand. "I appreciate this," he said. "Patrick told me how incredible the food is here; he says you're a fantastic chef."

"I'll do my best," the other man said with a smile. "I'm having my sister wait on you tonight, so I can vouch for her discretion. Enjoy your meal."

"I wish I had dressed up a little," Holly said, leaning towards him. "I feel very underdressed in jeans."

"You look perfect," Liam said. He reached for her hand across the table, happy when she accepted.

"Thank you," she said, ducking her head slightly. "I'm trying hard to battle the insecurity I feel when I'm around you."

"Please don't," he said. "I'm really enjoying your company and can honestly tell you that I don't think I've ever felt this way about someone before."

"Are you sure I'm not—"

"What?"

"Someone to pass two boring weeks in Vermont with?" She stared at the table as she finished the question, and he realized that she really did think that was a possibility. Despite all the time they had spent together and the kisses they had shared under the Christmas tree, she was still doubting him.

"Absolutely not," he said vehemently. "Everything with you is different. I have never been with a woman whom I missed when we weren't together, whom I couldn't stop thinking about. And you are all I can think of every second we aren't together. And when we are together, I'm thinking about how we can stay that way."

"Really?"

"Yes, really. If it wasn't, I wouldn't be saying all of this because I know it would just end up in a magazine or gossip page on social media. I usually keep things very light on purpose, so no one can get too close to me, but you make me want to take that risk. Please tell me this isn't one-sided because this is the most vulnerable I've ever felt," he said with a half-laugh.

"It's not. I have these waves of disbelief because of who you are, but I very much feel the same way," she admitted. "And Jake warned me that a picture already got out of us together when we were shopping. It just adds to my insecurity."

"I'm sorry, no one told me," he said. "But I try not to care what the public thinks about my life, if I can help it."

"It does make me worry about what people will say when I go back to my regular life, but I can ignore it," she said. "It helps that I don't know what happens after this."

"This being the holidays?"

"Yes." She nodded. "What do you plan to do?"

"Honestly, I have no idea. I was supposed to go home to California, but the more time I spend here, the less I want to go."

The waitress interrupted to deliver their drink orders and an appetizer that Wyatt had sent out for them. While she was there, Liam carefully considered his next words. Would it be coming on too strong to ask Holly to stay longer in Windsor Peak? Or to travel with him when he had to go overseas?

"What are you thinking?" Holly asked, taking a sip of her drink while waiting for his answer.

"That I don't want this to end," he said slowly. "Whatever it is that's developing between us, I want to see where it can go. You make me happy, and I hope I do the same. I find myself picturing a time when we would make decisions together, but I also don't want to rush whatever this is. Does that make sense?"

"Yes," she said with a nod. "It's barely been a week, although it feels like we've known each other for months. I'm excited about what might happen, but we don't need to rush into anything."

He grinned at her, squeezing her hand lightly. "I guess that means I'm up for more of your Christmas Craziness."

"Definitely not the name." She laughed. "But yes. What else did we have on the list? We've accomplished a lot, and I definitely feel like you're in the spirit. Maybe we can decorate cookies?"

"That sounds delicious," he agreed. "I do have one thing pestering me that I was hoping to get your help with."

"What is it?"

"There's a little boy who comes to the youth center. His name is Robbie. The first day, he came in sneakers with holes in them, a jacket too small, and even his clothes looked too small. I talked to the director, and she told me that his family has fallen on hard times and they're living with his grandparents," he told her. "They try to send extra food home to help the family, and I got him set up with new boots, a jacket, hat, and gloves. But I feel like I should be doing more."

"We did talk about how you can't save everyone," she said gently.

"I know, but I heard his dad is out of work," he said. "I was thinking I could get in touch with him, see if I could give him a job at the house? I need a caretaker anyway, especially with how much I'll be gone from here. They could live in one of the cottages out back. I was debating doing an apartment, but they don't have full kitchens. It will probably be better to redo them and either have them as guest suites or just part of the main house. I haven't really thought about it much yet. I'll run it by Jake and see what he thinks, but I did walk through the cottages and they are in good shape."

"I didn't go through them at all," she said. "I forgot they were even there."

"They are." He nodded. "Towards the back of the property but close enough to the house to run over if there was a problem. They would be rented out for guests attending events here, and I guess they were very popular in the ski season for rentals. Two bedrooms, a full kitchen, and probably more space than they have right now in the grandparents' house."

"I think that's amazingly generous of you," she said. "But before you commit one hundred percent to this idea, I think you need to meet them. What if there's more going on than you know about? Trusting the wrong person to oversee your investment would be a bad idea."

"You're right," he said. "I did see the dad briefly when he picked Robbie up, and he looked like a nice guy. Quiet, and kept to himself rather than talk to the other parents, but it could be the circumstances. I could try and pull him aside when he comes tomorrow to talk to him."

"Better yet…" Holly said. "Why not ask Ben Burrows for help? He knows everyone in town and is probably familiar with the family. I would guess he can give you enough information to know if this is a good idea and help you coordinate a meeting."

"You're brilliant," he said, beaming at her. "I'll call Ben in the morning."

"You are definitely my prize student in the Christmas class," she said, smiling at him. "You'll get an A for sure, with all this giving."

"I do like to help, especially when it's not being asked for," he said. "I feel like most of the time people come to me with a sob story, it's to take advantage of me in some way. Not all the time but a lot. That makes me less willing to get involved, but if I see something I can fix, why not? Normally, I swear people to secrecy or have them sign something, so they can't tell anyone."

"Why? So no one else comes to ask?"

"That." He nodded. "It does make me look like an easy target. But, also, I have a bad boy image in Hollywood that I need to maintain."

"Badboy or playboy?"

He hung his head slightly, feeling ashamed of how he had behaved for the first time since he got famous. All the women, the parties, and the frivolous spending without a lot of charity was not a good look, but it was as if a flip had switched when he came to Windsor Peak. Suddenly, all he wanted was one woman, a quiet night at home, and to help everyone. He wasn't sure if it was Holly, the town, the holiday, or seeing Natalie so broken that was changing him, or maybe a combination of them all. Either way, he hoped the changes were permanent.

"Both," he finally admitted. "I would encourage you not to google me, but I feel like you probably already did."

"Trust me, I closed it pretty quickly," she said, laughing. "But I did realize that the version of you in front of me is the one that I need to believe in. Not the one I see on the movie screen or my Google search."

"Good," he said softly. "Because I want to be the man worthy of you. I just might need some directions along the way."

"Speaking of directions…" she said, glancing up at him from under her eyelashes. "Where are we headed after this?"

"I happen to know of a private spot with a Christmas tree," he said. "We have our gingerbread village to create, and I made sure there was a fresh bottle of wine and firewood ready to go. But I should warn you that if I have another glass of wine when we get there, I probably won't be able to drive you home."

"Sounds perfect." She smiled at him again, and he felt his heart thump even louder.

He was falling in love with her, and even just admitting that to himself was the scariest thing he had ever done.

Chapter 16

"Where are you right now?"

Shea's voice broke through Holly's daydreams, and she laughed self-consciously. "Sorry, what did you say?"

"I asked if you were planning to go to the festival opening tomorrow night? Or the breakfast with Santa with all of us Saturday morning?"

"Oh, I hadn't really thought about it," Holly admitted. "I feel bad, like I haven't spent much time with you at all since I got here."

"You have," Shea argued. "Besides, it's nice to see you falling in love."

"What? What are you talking about?" Holly knew her voice sounded hysterical, but it matched how she felt on the inside.

Shea calmly stirred some creamer into her coffee and sighed. "Holly, you and Liam have been inseparable since you got here," she said. "And I know full well that you snuck in here very early this morning. Which we appreciate, so we wouldn't have to lie to Charlie. Of course, he was up and out for hockey practice before you got home, so you kind of wasted that early wakeup."

"Why were you awake?"

"Hello, baby? I have an infant who wants to eat hourly." Shea laughed. "Especially when her daddy and big brother are getting up to leave for the day. She seems to know she has to wake up and see them."

"So, the whole family knew I wasn't here?" Holly groaned, hiding her face in her hands.

"No." Shea laughed. "I didn't tell them. Well, I told Jake, and he thought it was great. He's worried or thinks he should be worried."

"Why?"

"Because he's never had a sister, and he doesn't know how this works. Should he ask Liam what his intentions are?"

"Oh, no. No, no, no. That would not be good."

"It might be just what you need," Shea said. "Or do you already know where it's headed?"

"I have no idea," Holly admitted. "We have fun together, and we seem to agree on all the major things. He makes me laugh, and he likes that I call him on his nonsense. But he's Liam Dorsey. And when this is over, he's going back to Hollywood to live his big life and I'll be at some random hospital in the Midwest."

"Do you need to be?"

"What do you mean?"

"You could go to California," Shea suggested. "You could work anywhere, really. And he also has no ties to California other than work, and from what Patrick says, they have months before they need to film again. Seems like you both have a lot of options if you just have a conversation about it."

"And how would I do that? 'Hey, Liam, I'm sure this isn't what you were thinking at all, but I'm kind of crazy about you.

And I was wondering if I could follow you back to California?'
I'm sure he would love that," Holly said with a dramatic eye roll.

"He might," Shea said gently. "You won't know unless you
try. If you are falling for him, let yourself be honest about that.
You don't have to wander the world alone. I worry about you,
and I know Mom and Dad do too."

"Really? It's not bad, honestly. I just like being able to see all
these places and have someone else pay for it. And I usually end
up with tons of time off," she said.

"But you have no roots. No landing pad if you have a bad
day and need a safe space," Shea said. "Having ties to the
community around you is important. You know I'd love for you
to settle up here near me or down south near Mom and Dad."

"I didn't realize it bothered you guys," she admitted. "I
don't know why I've liked it for so long. It settled me in a strange
way because it was challenging."

"Because it took all your focus and you didn't have to think
about yourself," Shea countered. "You've always been someone
who worries more about others than yourself. You'd rather give
someone your time than take theirs. The idea of being
somewhere that you might be form ties to would probably take
a toll on you emotionally, but it's worth it if you find your place.
Having people around you who will build you up and lean on
you is what life is about. You probably wouldn't have come here
if I hadn't had Izzie and insisted, because you would have
worried that you would be extra work for me. But in reality, I
just love having you here. I suspect you might be a little afraid
of settling down, so the constant movement keeps that from
getting the best of you."

"Wow," Holly whispered. "That was a lot."

"It was a long-winded way of saying that you should trust your heart," Shea said gently. "If you are in love with him, take a chance on it. If you want to stay here, or follow him, or build a life somewhere, don't let fear stop you."

***

"Christmas karaoke is tonight," Holly said as she piped frosting onto a gingerbread man.

"I heard," Liam answered. His brow was furrowed as he focused on putting buttons down his cookie, and he groaned when he put the last one on. "That's not straight."

"You're worried that someone will judge your cookie for having a crooked sweater vest?"

"I thought this would be so much easier than it is," he said. "Why do they make it look easy?"

"So that you'll buy the kits." She laughed. "If people knew it was this hard and frustrating, they wouldn't do it."

"Mr. Liam," a little voice called. Holly looked over to see Robbie poising a tube of frosting over a cookie. "You need to do it like this." The little boy drew a crooked line down the middle of his cookie, then beamed at Liam.

"Is that a—"

"It's a zipper! Then you don't have to think about buttons," Robbie said. "Buttons are hard."

"Tell Ms. Holly," Liam said. "She's making fun of me."

120

"That's not nice," the boy said, frowning at Holly. "My teacher said we should be nice to each other, even when we see our friends make a mistake."

Liam stuck his tongue out quickly at Holly while the boy wasn't looking, and she had to laugh.

"About the karaoke," she continued.

"What about it? I heard that we shouldn't expect to sing because Patrick and Jake basically just do a show, and no one else wants to sing after they do. Patrick was on Broadway and Jake claims he's even better, so no one even wants them to leave the stage," he said. "Which is fine with me. I'm happy to sit in the corner and work on a bottle of wine with you."

"We're going together?"

"Aren't we?" He looked up at her, a confused look on his face. "I'm sorry, should I have asked you? I just assumed since we had talked about it so much."

"No, it's fine," she said quickly. "What time is good for you to go?"

He glanced at his watch, then back at her. "Do you want to run back to Shea's, get ready, and I'll pick you up there in an hour? Then we only have one car, so I can steal you again for the night. But I'm not getting up at five to drive you home tomorrow morning. We're adults and shouldn't have to worry."

"I know, it's just Charlie I'm thinking about," she said.

"Can't Charlie think you're sleeping in?"

"Sure," she said. "He honestly probably won't notice anyway."

"Right." He grinned at her. "I'm sure it's the last thing he wants to think about. Actually, second to last. His dad and Shea would be the last."

"I think Ben and Stella might be higher than me on the list of things not to think about." She laughed.

"See? No big deal. Now, we can have breakfast together and make plans for the weekend," he said.

"The festival starts tomorrow night," she said. "And then the ball is on Saturday."

"That's right," he said, snapping his fingers. "I need to make sure we have everything in place to move the walls and tables."

He pulled out his phone and started texting, and she held in a sigh. She had been hoping that he would mention the two of them attending the ball together, but he was either assuming they would, like he did for karaoke, or he had no intention of going with her. Hopefully, the night out with everyone would shed some light on the mystery.

She drove back to Shea's house slowly, the roads covered with a fresh coating of snow and requiring extra care. Shea and Jake had already left, with the plan to drop the baby and Charlie off at Dan's house for Ben and Stella to watch. Charlie didn't require babysitting, but the extra set of hands with the babies and Calle would come in handy, and the teen was always willing to help. Shea had texted her as she was driving, explaining their plan and that they had all packed overnight bags in case the snow got heavier, so they wouldn't have to drive back in the snow with the baby. The weather had solved her own problem of sleeping elsewhere since no one would be home to notice.

As she showered to get ready for the night, Shea's words rattled around in her head. Everyone here in Windsor Peak seemed to be settled and happy in their relationships, and loved the community they lived in. It did make her think about the sacrifices she'd made in keeping herself so isolated, and what she had missed out on. Perhaps Liam was someone worth fighting for, or maybe it would just inspire her to search out her own happiness. She didn't dare allow her heart to hope that Liam would fall in love with her, despite how quickly she found herself falling for him.

Chapter 17

Robbie was pulling on his coat when Liam came out of the backroom, where he had been discussing the logistics of the weekend with the staff. They had coordinated volunteers to come set up the space in the morning, and then the catering staff would take over. Zoe was in charge, as her and Kendra's catering company had been able to take over the tasks. Kendra reported that Zoe ran a tight ship and would have the place ready well before the opening.

The offer to move the ball had been met with huge thanks from the mayor and the manager of the inn, who was relieved to free up the room that night. Apparently, it had been double booked, and they had been scrambling to find a solution when Holly had approached him. It would be interesting to see the space Liam was now used to seeing filled with kids and various activities now decorated in finery, but he'd seen stranger things in his life.

"Hey, Robbie," he called. "I'll walk you out."

The little boy chattered as they walked out, talking about everything he had done since the school day had ended. He thrived in the open setting of the youth center, where he could explore his many interests without restrictions or the need to sit still. When they got out to the driveway, Liam saw Robbie's father standing next to a beat-up SUV. Ben Burrows had approved of the choice and encouraged Liam to approach him, and swore he would keep Liam's secret for the time being.

"Hi, I'm Liam," he said to the man, offering his hand.

"Robert," he said, shaking with a firm grasp. "Nice to meet you. Robbie talks about you all the time."

"Same. I've heard a lot of great things about you," Liam said. He waited while Robert got his son into the back seat of the SUV and shut the door before continuing. "I hope I'm not overstepping, but I heard that you were looking for work. I'm in need of someone to manage this property for me since I won't be around all the time. And even when I am, there are things that I don't want to deal with, like how you possibly mow a lawn this size. I heard you worked as a warehouse manager up in Burlington?"

"I did," he said. "But I ran into some problems, and I've had some trouble finding work. My wife was sick, and I needed to be around for Robbie. But things are better now."

"I know it doesn't seem like it now, but there was a time that I needed a break," Liam said. "I do understand how you're feeling right now, believe it or not. If you're interested, we could talk more about the job here. There are a few cottages down by the tree line, and you would be welcome to live in one of those. I'd actually prefer it, so there is someone here when I'm not. You'd be in charge of making sure the people doing things, like landscaping or plowing, show up and the bills get to my accountant. Basic repairs around the house, which you can hire out if you're not handy. It's a lot of property, and overseeing everything is a full-time job."

"It sounds similar to what I did at the warehouse," Robert said slowly. "Just a different setting. But making sure that deliveries go where they should, staff arrives and does their job, that all suits me."

"Perfect," Liam said with a grin. "Why don't I have my manager reach out to you to discuss the finer details. Salary, benefits, all that. I'll warn you now that they'll ask you to sign something stating that you won't report anything here to the press, but I feel like I can count on your discretion."

"Absolutely. There is no chance I would risk ruining this opportunity for my family."

"Speaking of, I heard your wife had been sick," Liam said. "I don't mean to intrude, but if there is anything I can do to help there, just let me know. I can get you in with some of the best doctors in the world."

"That's very generous of you," Robert responded. "But she's doing good now. She had a battle for a while with breast cancer, that's what put us behind. Her health was more important than anything else, and I can admit that I missed some work taking her to treatments. But she's doing well now and getting stronger every day, got a clean bill of health just the other day."

"That's great news. And I absolutely agree, your family takes precedence over any job, even here. Let me get your number," Liam said, pulling out his own phone. "I'll text you his info, so you'll have it as well, just in case my number stops working one day. I have to change it a lot, but you can always get in touch with my manager, and he can give you the new one."

Robert looked at the ground as if he was afraid to make eye contact. When he finally looked up, Liam could tell he was battling strong emotions. "If you'd be willing to give me a chance, I'd take excellent care of this place," he said. "I could never thank you enough for the opportunity."

"No need to thank me," Liam said. "For all you know, I could turn into a nightmare."

The other man laughed, and they shook hands before Robert got into his car to drive Robbie home. Liam had encouraged him to come back the next morning with his wife to see the cottage and told him to start moving in whenever he was ready. As he watched them drive away, his first thought was that he couldn't wait to tell Holly about this.

***

Liam had relocated to one of the apartments attached to the main house after having a conversation with his friends about it. Natalie had agreed that it wasn't a problem for him to live down the street, and he had offered her the apartment on the opposite side of the house. A change of scenery might be just what she needed, and he hoped that she would take him up on the offer. She had seemed to be considering it, assuming he went through with the promise of adding a security system. He had immediately texted his assistant, asking him to get to work on a system that would oversee the entire house but also have individual systems for each apartment. He had also talked to Jake about doing some quick renovations on the side he wanted Nat to take, to make it more comfortable for her. Now, he was happy to have his belongings there, so he could quickly shower and get ready for karaoke and have some time to set up a few things in the hopes for later in the night before he left to pick Holly up.

He drove the short distance to Jake's house, enjoying the view of all the Christmas decorations in town. Each house glowed, with lights trimming the outside and the bushes, and Christmas trees shining in the windows. It was snowing lightly, and the entire experience was like living inside of a snow globe. He'd never envisioned himself as a small-town kind of guy but, apparently, he was. He had already made the decision to stay after the holidays and hoped he could convince Holly to do the same.

Everything had been so perfect for them, other than their disastrous first meeting. This was the first time he'd met anyone like her before and certainly never felt this way before. Falling in love so quickly had caught him by surprise, but Natalie had called him out on it, and she was right. Once he opened himself up to the possibility, he realized he couldn't envision the future without her. He wanted to end the days with her, tell her funny stories about things he encountered, and get her advice on things that challenged him.

Holly answered the door on his first knock, and he laughed instantly. She was wearing the most ridiculous, ugly, hilarious sweater that he had ever seen. It depicted a fireplace on the front, lit by tiny lights sewn into the fabric. Actual tiny stockings hung from the mantle, swinging as she walked.

She put her hands on her hips and stared at him, pointing at his own black sweater. "You know this is an ugly Christmas sweater thing."

"I don't think I did." He laughed. "But I'm okay with that."

"Absolutely not," she said. "I had a sense this might happen, so I got you a present." She disappeared into the kitchen, returning with a bag in her hands.

He shook his head and held up his hands. "No," he tried. "If I put whatever that is on, it will be on the cover of a magazine, declaring me the worst dressed in Hollywood."

"But you aren't in Hollywood," she pointed out. "Most likely, no one will take your picture. And you don't want to disappoint me."

"Everyone said tonight will be crazy busy," he said. "The festival kicks off tomorrow, so tourists will be there. Someone is bound to take a picture and send it to TMZ."

"If that's the worst thing that could happen to you today, you're pretty lucky," she said. She hesitated, and he saw something ripple across her face that he couldn't catch. "Unless the issue is being photographed with me? Ruining your bachelor image?"

"Absolutely not," he said. "Give it to me."

The sweater was equally as bad as hers, but in his lit-up fireplace scene, Santa's legs hung down from the chimney. He pulled off the black sweater he had, hearing Holly sigh as he did, and pulled the ugly one on. "I think you did that for the show," he said, pulling her towards him. "I would have taken my shirt off if you asked."

"It's just a lot of muscle," she said. "And it's hard to get used to."

He kissed her, then made her laugh as he started backing her towards the stairs. "Let me guess, you also want to be punctual?" he said as she pulled away.

"Yes, and I know you don't want everyone talking about how you arrived late and disheveled." She laughed. "Let's go."

He followed Holly's direction, to pull around the back of the restaurant so they could sneak in through the kitchen door. As predicted, the restaurant was packed, but Kendra had set up the room so that a table was isolated enough that Patrick, Liam, and Natalie would be left alone. Nat was tucked into the table between the gigantic Mike and the equally imposing Jake, where no one could get close to her. Rex was on the floor under the table, at Jake's feet, and from what Liam could tell, seemed to be giving Natalie as much comfort as he did Jake.

Liam pulled out a chair next to Shea for Holly before settling in himself. He felt eyes on him from every corner of the room and suddenly felt uncomfortable. While he wanted to put his arm around the back of her chair or pull her closer, he knew what that would look like the next morning on the gossip sites. He didn't want her to have to deal with the scrutiny or the nasty comments online, so he purposely turned to talk to Dan. When Jake and Patrick got up to sing, he excused himself and slid into the empty seat next to Natalie. The duo sang for nearly two hours, doing every holiday song the crowd yelled out to them, including Mariah Carey's song, which brought the crowd to its feet.

When they finally came off the stage, everyone at the table was ready to leave. The new parents were anxious to get back to their infants, and Natalie had hit her limit of being out. Mike had offered to take her home several times, and as Jake and Patrick were taking their bows, she used the opportunity to sneak out the back door with the trainer. Liam moved back over to Holly's side but noticed the stiffness in her shoulders.

"You ready to go?" he asked, leaning over to say it into her ear.

"I'll just have Jake drop me off at the house," she answered. "It's snowing. You should get home."

"What did I do?" he asked. When she didn't answer, he moved closer. "Please tell me what I did wrong."

"I thought this was a night for us to be together," she said. "And you very clearly didn't want to be seen with me. It's okay; I get it. You're a movie star, and I'm not. It makes sense that you'd go sit with Natalie."

"First of all, you know there is nothing between Nat and me," he said. "I only moved there because she looked so nervous when Jake got up. Second, not being seen with you has absolutely nothing to do with you. Well, it does. But not like you think. Please, let me explain. Come home with me, and we can talk."

"I think I'll pass," she said, standing and pulling her jacket on. "After all, the picture that went viral of us buying Christmas decorations had people questioning your sanity to be seen with someone like me. I just didn't realize how quickly you would shut me out for the sake of your image."

He watched her walk out, feeling like his heart was cracking. It had never occurred to him that by trying to protect her privacy, he would destroy her confidence in him. And possibly destroy any chance they had of a future.

Chapter 18

"I just don't get it," Holly fumed, pacing in her sister's kitchen. It had been a full day since the disastrous karaoke night, and she hadn't heard anything from Liam since she left the bar. She had attended the first night of the festival and enjoyed the breakfast with Santa that Kendra had held at the Windsor Palace but hadn't caught sight of Liam once.

"What has he said since?"

"Not a whole lot," Holly said. "Just that I had the wrong impression, and he wants the chance to explain. He texted that Thursday night, and nothing since. I didn't answer."

"I think that's fair of him to want to talk," Shea said softly. "Don't you?"

"Don't take his side."

"I'm not, I promise. But it just doesn't fit who he is and how he has acted. You aren't someone to be embarrassed of, and I just don't see that being the truth," Shea said.

"What else could it be? Everything was fine, and then he ignored me all night. But wanted me to go home with him," Holly said. "I really have been nothing but a holiday hookup for him."

The doorbell rang, and Jake called out that he would get it. Holly stared into her coffee mug glumly, trying to figure out how to tell her sister that she couldn't possibly stay in Windsor Peak. Christmas and her birthday with Liam just down the street was not an option she could handle; she needed to leave as soon as possible. She had spent half the night scouring the options for nursing positions with her travel company, but every one had been wrong for some reason or another. She refused to admit that what was wrong with all of them was that they weren't a small town in Vermont. Or near a certain city in California that a movie star would live.

"Holly, you have a delivery," Jake called out. He walked into the kitchen, carrying a large, flat box that was tied with a giant red bow.

"What is it?" She stood, walking over to where he had placed it on the table.

"No idea." He shrugged. "It was FedEx. There's a note there."

She pulled the card off the box, noting it was addressed to her at Shea's address. The outside of the card was blank, but on the inside, a note was written in unfamiliar handwriting.

For the Holiday Ball.

The ribbon came undone with a simple pull, and she lifted the lid off and gasped.

"What is it?" Shea asked from behind her.

Holly finished peeling the tissue paper back, revealing the top half of the gown before pulling it from the box. It was a gorgeous green that shimmered in the overhead lights as if sparkles were sewn in. On a closer look, she could see the silver strings subtly laced through the bodice and more in the skirt.

The sweetheart neckline led to small straps that looked as if they would hang off each shoulder, with clear straps hidden to hold it up. The back dipped low, and the skirt billowed just enough to make her think she would feel like a princess in this dress.

"It's perfect," Shea breathed. "I'm insanely jealous right now."

"Why would he do this?"

"Who?" Jake asked, pouring a coffee and watching the two women.

"Liam," they said in unison.

"I guess he wants to go to the ball with you," Jake said with a shrug. "Right? I thought you would have already made those plans."

"I wonder when he did this," Shea said. "You'll have to answer his texts now."

"No, I won't," Holly said stubbornly. "Maybe you should wear this."

"I'm four inches shorter and just had a baby," Shea said. "No chance I'm wearing that. I have a black dress that will cover my waistline."

"Your waistline is perfect," Jake said, coming over to kiss his wife on the cheek.

"That dress was made for you," Shea said. "If you don't wear it, you're a fool."

***

Holly pretended as though she wasn't going to wear the dress, but it was a futile exercise. From her first glimpse, she had fallen in love with the beautiful garment, and it was only confirmed when she slid it on after her shower that evening. After taking her time showering, applying makeup, and styling her hair in a simple updo, she had stood gazing at her options. A simple red dress that she had planned to wear hung next to the gifted gown on the door to her closet, but her hands had pulled the green one on instead. It slid on her body easily, the material caressing her skin. When she turned to look in the mirror before zippering, she sighed, knowing nothing she ever wore again would suit her like this dress. The green made her eyes pop and seemed to highlight her pale skin and the copper highlights in her hair.

"Oh, my," Shea said from the doorway. "That dress is a piece of art. Here, turn around and I'll zip it."

She turned and let Shea raise the zipper, confirming that it was a perfect fit. "How did he do this?"

"No idea," Shea said. "But I'm glad he did. Mom and Dad are here; they are watching the babies tonight while we all go to the ball. Come down when you're ready."

Holly picked up the heels she would wear, not willing to put them on one minute earlier than needed, and the small purse that she had transferred the essentials into, before heading down the stairs. Her parents were on the couch, each holding a baby, while Dan, Kendra, Jake, and Shea looked on anxiously.

Jake whistled as she came down, making the others look up. "Looking good," Jake said with a grin.

"Good doesn't describe it," Kendra said. "Please don't stand too close to me; you're gorgeous."

"So are—"

Kendra interrupted Dan with a laugh and a kiss. "Save it," she said. "You still get credit, but don't take away from how she looks."

"You look fantastic," Dan said to Holly, putting his arm around Kendra. "Are we all ready?"

The doorbell rang before they could put coats on, and they all glanced at each other in confusion.

Shea opened the door, accepting a wrapped package before quickly closing it on the cold air. "I think this is for you," she said, holding the small box out to Holly.

"What could this possibly be?" The box was wrapped identically to the gown, right down to the ribbon and small card with her name on it. The card read:

Only you could outshine this. It goes with the dress.

The ribbon fell off easily, and the lid revealed a silver necklace with an emerald encircled by diamonds that were shaped like a snowflake.

"Beautiful," Shea whispered. "Here, let me put it on you."

"This is all too much," Holly objected. "I can't accept this."

Dan shook his head. "You also can't refuse because that would be insulting to him. Take it as the gift that it is, with the thought that it comes from his heart."

"He's right," Kendra said. "If you want a future with him, showing up with all of this on shows that. If you don't, then change and send a message that way."

"Do you, honey?" Her mom's voice piped in from behind her. "Do you love him?"

"I do," she finally admitted. "But I don't think it's enough."

"My darling girl," her dad said, his deep voice soothing. "It's more than enough. It's everything."

"Whatever the problem is," her mom said, "go fix it."

Holly slid into the back of the SUV that was warming up outside, happy to be alone in the third row so she could gather her thoughts. Jake was behind the wheel, Rex settled into the space between the two captain's seats behind him. The two couples were anxious about leaving the babies again and were already discussing how early they could leave, so she could tune out.

Obviously, the gifts were from Liam; that was clear. No one else could have sent them to her, and yet the timing was off. She was mad at him and trying to ignore the feelings that she had. If she were to admit it, she was using the events at karaoke to give her an out. The insecurities that plagued her as she got to know him, thinking that she wasn't enough for him, had won out. As soon as she had the slightest thought that he didn't want to be seen with her, she had jumped on it.

If she had to examine her heart, she knew she was falling in love. Maybe already had fallen. It was the most terrifying feeling and yet the most glorious. She thought back to the two years before, hearing Shea's excitement when Jake returned from Afghanistan and then when they started dating. She had been so happy for her sister, but a small part of her had wondered if it would ever happen for her. And yet, when it did, the first response she had was to ruin it as quickly as possible.

Now, she had just minutes to decide if she was brave enough to go after what she wanted and make this the most unforgettable Christmas ever, or if she was going to take the role of the Grinch and hide her heart away.

Chapter 19

Liam paced behind the small stage, where the mayor had agreed to let him hide out. Apparently, word had gotten out that Liam had purchased the property that was being used as the youth center, courtesy of the former owner who still had ties to the town, and everyone wanted to thank him personally. He didn't mind speaking to everyone, but he was so worried about whether Holly would come to the event and if she would be wearing his gifts, it had made it hard to focus. The mayor had seen something was distracting him and kindly offered the space for him to gather his thoughts.

"Dan texted that they're almost here," Patrick said, stepping behind the curtain. "You ready?"

"I think I've lost my mind," Liam admitted. "What am I doing?"

"Telling the woman you love how you feel? Seems like a solid plan," Patrick said. He wrapped an arm around Emma, who had followed him, before continuing. "Worked out well for me."

"But you were made for this. You've wanted to be in a relationship since I met you," he said. "I've been playing the field ever since we met. And before that, no one really wanted anything to do with me. Now, they just want to be seen with me; they don't care who I am."

"She does," Emma said gently. "She's not like the women you've been with. Just be honest with her and with yourself."

"She's right, as always," Patrick said. "You deserve happiness. And while we're on the subject, I'm glad to hear that you'll be my neighbor here. I don't know why you didn't tell us that you bought the house."

"I didn't want to make it about me," Liam explained. "But I really like it here."

"Good," Patrick grinned. "We like having you here. And not wanting something to be about you is a major change for the better. I think Holly is a good influence on you. Speaking of, we should get out there."

Liam followed his friend through the curtain, blinking when the bright lights hit his eyes. The band was just starting to play as the doors opened, and he saw her. Holly stood, the bright Christmas lights strung around the room shining on her, as her eyes searched the room. They stopped when they met his, and without thinking, he started across the room towards her. She met him halfway, in the center of the dance floor, stopping an arm's length away.

"You look beautiful," he said. "Even better than I imagined. I hope you liked the dress."

"It's the nicest thing I've ever worn," she said, looking down at the dress. "I have no idea how you pulled it off."

"I called a woman we work with in California; she's helped Patrick out several times. She had me send a picture of you, and Shea gave her your sizes," he said. She shot a look at her sister, who shrugged at her with a smile. "She had it shipped out yesterday and promised that it would be here in time."

"You just did this yesterday? Why?"

"Because I needed to say that I'm sorry," he said. "I handled everything wrong at karaoke night. I should have told you that my biggest worry was that any pictures posted would put you in the public eye. That I can handle anything they say about me, but if they went after you, I wouldn't know how to handle that. The internet is a nasty place, where people feel free to say things they would never say to your face, and I couldn't imagine putting you there without you knowing what was happening. I had no idea there were already pictures out, or that you had seen anything. I was just trying to protect you."

"I didn't think of that," Holly said. "It did make me feel wildly insecure to be compared to the women you've dated in the past. I just thought you didn't want to ruin your image any more than it had been when that picture came out."

"Trust me when I say that you could only enhance my image." He laughed. "Having a woman like you be by my side would be the best thing for me. But that doesn't matter to me at all."

"It doesn't?" She looked disappointed, so he rushed to explain.

"Not like that. I want you to be by my side, but not to change how the public views me. I want you there because I feel like it's where you belong. And because you make me happy and make me feel things I never thought I would feel."

"Ditto," she said with a smile.

"And for the record, you're the most gorgeous woman I've ever seen," he said. "If you could see yourself through my eyes, whether it's tonight in this amazing dress or in your hideous Christmas sweater, I think you're beautiful. But even more important, I think you're one of the best people I've ever met. I want to be the man you deserve, and to be called out when I act like an entitled jerk."

"You don't do that as much anymore," she said with a smile. "Not since the first day."

"That's because of you," he said. "When I got here, I honestly didn't know who I was. Seeing myself through your eyes helped me get comfortable in my own skin. If someone like you can see good in me, I can't be all bad. All these years of Hollywood and being surrounded by people who really didn't care about me as a person made me unsure of myself in every situation."

"I never would have guessed that you were insecure in any way," Holly said.

"I hid it well. But I questioned everything I did and played this arrogant character when I was off balance in a situation."

"That would explain our first meeting," she laughed. "And the second."

"I never think people will want to be around Liam, the guy who was a no one for a lot of his life," he explained. "Going from being a nothing to being a huge celebrity takes some adjusting, and I wasn't doing well with it before I met you."

"I don't think you were ever a no one," she said gently. "And I promise to stop googling your past since I know the true you."

"You really do. Maybe more than I know myself, I'd say," he admitted. "I'll count on you calling me out when I'm falling back onto my old habits. But I think the changes are going to stick. You helped me appreciate my friends even more than I did, and respect how hard my parents worked all their lives. You shared your love of Christmas with me and made me love it. You inspired me to help with the youth center. The old me would have just ignored the problem entirely. You inspire me to do good things and to be happy."

"You were quite the Grinch," she laughed. "I'm glad I won you over."

"More than that," he said. He felt the nerves in his stomach, but knew he had to keep moving forward. "You made me believe in love. You have my heart, Holly. I've been miserable since we left the Palace that night, wanting to fix things with you. I love being with you, and I look forward to seeing you when we're apart. I never thought I would feel this way, be this crazy about someone. But you're someone I want a future with, and I'll follow you anywhere you want to go."

"It's funny you say that," Holly said. "I spent all day yesterday looking at job options, and nothing appealed to me. I haven't had a true home since I was a kid, and I've been happy to wander around alone. I didn't have to risk being hurt because I wouldn't let anyone close. But ever since you spilled coffee all over me, you have turned my world upside down. I'm crazy about you too, and I'm sorry I tried to push you away."

He pulled her into his arms and kissed her, then held her close and started moving to the music. "I love you, Holly. I know it's fast to say that, but it's the truth."

"I love you too, Liam," she said. "I can't believe this is happening, but I have never been happier than I am at this moment, right now."

"I moved into the apartment at the house," he said suddenly. "Will you come there with me? I want to show you something."

"Okay," she said. "Although, I'd like to enjoy this ball with our friends and family for a little while if you don't mind. And let people see this dress; it would be a shame to not let this dress enjoy a party."

"Whatever you want," he said, smiling down at her. He could wait any length of time for her, as long as they had something to look forward to together.

They danced and socialized with the people of the small town and mingled with tourists who stopped to meet Liam. The night passed quickly, and before he knew it, he was helping Holly put on her coat and leading her out into the fresh snow. The Christmas lights they had hung lit up the house as they approached, but she slowed down as the snow got higher. He quickly realized what was happening and scooped her into his arms, carrying her to the porch.

"What are you doing?" She laughed.

"You have heels on, and they haven't been shoveling up here," he explained. "This is faster."

He carefully placed her on the porch and then opened the door, stepping back to let her in first. She gasped as she walked in, and he entered behind her, seeing it through her eyes. He had transformed the space into a winter wonderland, starting with the Christmas tree in the corner that they had decorated together. He had expanded on it, adding garland and candles around the room, which were battery operated and on a timer to save him from burning the house down. Mistletoe dangled overhead, and two stockings hung from the mantle. One with his name on it, the other hers. She walked over and traced the letters on the stocking before turning back to him, tears in her eyes.

"You did all this for me?"

"I did," he said. "I had planned to bring you back here after karaoke, to tell you how I felt. But then things went wrong, so I added even more to it in the hopes you would come here tonight. I know it's fast, but I think this is meant to be our holiday home."

"That's what we should have been calling it," she said tearfully.

"What?"

"Your seasonal training." She laughed. "Or rather, our training, because it turns out I needed to have my eyes opened too. Holiday home. I can't imagine being anywhere unless you're there with me, so you're my home. I learned that I do want roots, and a person to rely on and grow with. And you found a place where you want to belong. We both got what we needed for Christmas this year."

"I'll be a believer from now on," he promised. "As long as I get to celebrate Christmas and every other holiday with you."

"Lucky for you, my birthday is coming up," she teased. "You get to experience your first birthday and Christmas all at once."

"I wouldn't want anything else," he whispered, pulling her close. He slid her jacket off and then hit a button on the remote to play music softly. As Bing Crosby sang about being home for Christmas, they danced slowly, and he found himself silently agreeing with the lyrics that there was no place he would rather be.

Acknowledgements

Jake's story will never feel complete to me, because it's what really started me on this journey. Throughout the series I've been able to weave in his battles with PTSD, and I wanted to find the perfect way to help him further. I heard about K9s for Warriors years ago, and I so admire the work they do. They are one of many organizations that help train these magnificent dogs to help our Veterans function in a healthy way, and I love that they work with rescues. It's like saving two lives in one act, and that alone moves me. If you're looking for a way to get involved, please visit their website.

I have to thank all of you who are reading these books. I say it every time, but you really are making my dreams come true. I am still amazed when I hold a book with my name on it, or when a stranger comes to a signing to meet me. I love doing Zoom's with book clubs to talk about the books, which allows me to connect with readers from all over the world. I hope to one day be able to do a wider book tour and meet you all in person, but I'm having a blast with the virtual hang outs!

A huge thank you to my parents, who are always my first readers, and who love these characters as much as I do. And to Jeff for his massive marketing campaigns on Facebook, and Danielle for being the best everything. My nephews and nieces, Brendan, Conor, Timmy, Tessa and Emmy, make me proud every day because of the amazing people they are.

I would list out my friends if I thought I would remember everyone to acknowledge – but we all know I'd forget someone and have to write a whole book with your name in it. Thank you all for the suggestions, for letting me use your names, and for reading.

And of course, the biggest thank you to my family – my husband Tom, who makes it possible for me to do this, and my boys, Camden and Calum. I'm so incredibly lucky to be living this life, and to have a healthy, happy family, and I never take it for granted. I'll freeze in any rink, or sit in the rain at a football game, if it means I get to watch my boys do what they love. And seeing them walk in to a signing (if you know my husband, you know a bookstore is the last place you might find him) or brag about my books to someone, shows me that it goes both ways and they would do anything for me. I love you all!

Merry Christmas and the Happiest of New Years to you all! I can't wait to see what will happen in Windsor Peak next year!

Stay Tuned

I am already working on book five – I'm sure you can take a guess who it will feature! Make sure to follow me on social media (@deniselathamwrites or links below) and sign up for my newsletter on my website (www.deniselatham.com) to be up to date on the latest news!

Facebook   **Instagram**

Amazon   **Goodreads**

I'd also be so grateful if you would leave a review of this book where you purchased it, or on Goodreads. The more reviews and shares that the books get, the more other readers can find them and fall in love with Windsor Peak!